Books by Lawrence Clark Powell

AN INTRODUCTION TO ROBINSON JEFFERS

ROBINSON JEFFERS, THE MAN AND HIS WORK

THE MANUSCRIPTS OF D. H. LAWRENCE

PHILOSOPHER PICKETT

ISLANDS OF BOOKS

LAND OF FICTION

THE ALCHEMY OF BOOKS

HEART OF THE SOUTHWEST

BOOKS WEST SOUTHWEST

A SOUTHWESTERN CENTURY

THE MALIBU (WITH W. W. ROBINSON)

A PASSION FOR BOOKS

A PASSION FOR BOOKS

A PASSION FOR BOOKS

LAWRENCE
CLARK
POWELL

CLEVELAND AND NEW YORK

THE WORLD PUBLISHING COMPANY

PUBLISHED BY The World Publishing Company
2231 West 110th Street, Cleveland 2, Ohio

PUBLISHED SIMULTANEOUSLY IN CANADA BY
Nelson, Foster & Scott Ltd.

Library of Congress Catalog Card Number: 59-5927

Acknowledgment is hereby made to those periodicals in which much of the material in this book first appeared.

Acknowledgment is made for permission to quote from the following:

Death Comes for the Archbishop by Willa Cather, copyright 1926, 1927 by Willa Cather, reprinted by permission of Alfred A. Knopf, Inc.

"Summer Holiday," from *Roan Stallion, Tamar and Other Poems*, by Robinson Jeffers, copyright 1925 by Boni & Liveright, Inc. and renewed 1953 by Robinson Jeffers, reprinted by permission of Random House, Inc.

"The Panther," from *Rilke: Selected Poems, with English Translations by C. F. MacIntyre*, by Rainer Maria Rilke, copyright 1940 by the University of California Press, reprinted by permission of the University of California Press.

Islandia by Austin Tappan Wright, copyright 1942 by Farrar & Rinehart, Inc., reprinted by permission of Rinehart & Company, Inc.

The woodcut on the title page is by Antonio Frasconi.

Second Printing
2HC359

Copyright © 1958 by Lawrence Clark Powell. All rights reserved. No part of this book may be reproduced in any form without written permission from the publisher, except for brief passages included in a review appearing in a newspaper or magazine. Printed in the United States of America.

To Fay

CONTENTS

PREFACE   11

Part One

MY FAVORITE FOUR-LETTER WORD; OR, HOW
    I FEEL ABOUT THE B——K   15

THE MAGNETIC FIELD   22

THE POWER TO EVOKE   40

THREE LOVES HAVE I   55

IN IT TOGETHER   70

EUCALYPTUS TREES AND LOST MANUSCRIPTS   79

STOP THIEF!   85

MY BIGGEST FLOP   92

ALL THAT IS POETIC IN LIFE   97

CONTENTS

Part Two

EDUCATION FOR ACADEMIC LIBRARIANSHIP	115
MITCHELL OF CALIFORNIA	134
THE EXCITEMENT OF ADMINISTRATION	144
LEARNING TO TEACH, TEACHING TO LEARN	151
LIBRARIANSHIP IS A CALLING	158
THE GIFT TO BE SIMPLE	170
FROM PRIVATE COLLECTION TO PUBLIC INSTITUTION	185
BOOKS WILL BE READ	203
BOOKMAN IN SEVEN-LEAGUE BOOTS	216
THROUGH THE BURNING GLASS	238

PREFACE

THESE ESSAYS on the art of librarianship were written from 1948 through 1957. Some were intended to be spoken to library conferences; others were meant only to be read; all have been revised more or less to give them unity in this book. It is difficult to find words to satisfy both eye and ear, and I have done the best I can.

They are concerned with practice and preaching, with doing and teaching, with joy in my chosen profession, and my desire to transmit the essence of what I have done and learned and felt to others. This is why one talks and writes and publishes, and the reward comes when someone far or near writes or says, "That is the way it has been for me too, only I could never find the words to express it."

The ten years have been rich years of travel, twice to Europe and many times around the United States, always because of books, meeting fellow bookmen in libraries and bookshops, on campuses and in cities and little places, collecting books, reading books, talking books, and living with the added intensity which books give to life.

He who loves not books will find these essays meaningless, but he who like myself cannot live a day without some contact with books—to him I address these essays on the art of librarianship.

A list of persons who have been helpful to me at home and abroad would fill several pages. Betty Rosenberg and Everett Moore must be singled out, however, for their perceptive and honest criticism has improved my writing in many places, and I am truly grateful.

L.C.P.

UCLA Library
University of California
Los Angeles
September 27, 1958

Part One

MY FAVORITE FOUR-LETTER WORD; OR, HOW I FEEL ABOUT THE B——K

HAPPY AM I with an ax-proof neck and a barb-thick skin, for I have been the target of both friend and foe; of well-meaning formers who wish I would stop writing in *my* personal way and start writing in their impersonal way, and of less cordial latters who also dislike the autobiographical mode—literary prudes who walk with Whittier not with Whitman; and by still others who say that I should restrain my sentimental feelings about books, thinkers who prefer the knowledge of the brain to the wisdom of the heart.

If I heeded these critics, I would stop writing, for it would be just too much work trying to be someone I am not. Wisdom lies in accepting the limitations of one's own nature, and in not seeking to emulate "this man's gift and that man's art." When younger, I foolishly wanted to

First published in the AB Bookman's Yearbook, *1956.*

be liked by everyone; now it is a tonic to be disliked by those to whom my way of life is anathema. I have never written a book or an essay, or compiled a bibliography, without being moved by the excitement that possesses me when I reach for a book. I was born crazy about books, and all my life has been a pleasant worsening of the state, from my earliest years in a small-town public library to my working life in great libraries all over the world and in bookshops and private collections. I believe in books, share Milton's respect for their sacred nature, earn my living as a bookman, and seek constantly to communicate my feelings to others, by example, by the spoken and written word, by "living with books," in the words of Helen E. Haines.

There is no moderate life for a bookman. Suspect is he who lives a bookish life from eight to five, then shuts the door to heaven-on-earth, and turns to cards or golf or worse. Give me the man whose life is encircled by books, who lives and plays, wakes and dreams, sells or lends, and everlastingly reads books, who practices what he preaches, the true gospel that, next to mother's milk, books are the best food. Thus I view with alarm the invasion of the book world by barbarians who neither believe in books for their totality of being, their fusion of form and content, nor have any sentimental feelings toward the book as a thing-in-itself.

After an address I gave in 1952 called "The Alchemy of Books," in which I deplored a trend toward the so-called nonbook materials, one of my friends chided me for confusing the contents of a book with its format. Only the former is important and lasting, he said; the latter is merely incidental. All a scholar wants is his text, whether it be a first edition or a reprint. Why all this fuss over originals? Are not the collector and the scholar an unmeeting twain?—the one moved solely by "condition" and a sense of rivalry, the other so indifferent to such matters as to accept his texts on sandwich wrappers, match covers, or filmed on the wall while he lies abed late o'Sundays.

Shades of Sadleir, of Wilmarth Lewis, Evans, Clark, De Golyer, and the rest of the scholar-collectors, whose passion for condition has meant the difference between this generation's having and not having the legacy of the past as it was originally fashioned!

There is no way of communicating with people who, by an imbalance of thinking over feeling, do not respond to the wedding of form and content which makes Milton in seventeenth-century calf or sheep infinitely more powerful than the great Puritan in Fabrikoid or on film. As if to say that Helen of Troy could have launched those ships or burned those towers by remote control, rather than by the presence of her face and form, by the soft words, the ringing words her sweet lips said.

If these come-now-no-nonsense-about-books boys had their way, they would outlaw the passion which moved Brown and Clements, Folger and Huntington to rear their useful monuments, and substitute the modular warehouse. It is proper to confer about the future of "the book," even to ask is the book obsolete, but when library school prospectuses are issued which run to thousands of words without once mentioning the word *book*, then the bounds of propriety have been exceeded. The appeal is to would-be housekeepers, analysts, probers, and planners, to unsocial scientists who can be led to literature but not made to read and who long to de-emphasize books, mechanize the library, and change its name to "materials center," a term more properly applied by anatomists to the dissecting room. We have documentalists, communications clerks, and media men who blank out when they hear the words *library, librarian, book,* and *reading*. In their concern with costs and size, they have lost contact with librarians to whom the only elements of librarianship worth any extended talk or study are books and people. To make a career of housekeeping, to confer and to publish and otherwise glorify the Cinderella aspects of our working life, is to degrade the art of librarianship and further to confirm what the public suspects, that this kind of librarianship is mere clerking, is book-keeping, is chorework.

And these pseudo librarians wonder why there is a problem in recruiting enough good people to enter library schools and train for the thousands of vacancies all over the world. One reason is that they do not know how to speak to the latent bookishness in young people, how to arouse and to feed the bookish hunger which God mysteriously goes on putting into a certain number of human beings in each generation, year after year, from the time of the first clay tablet and papyrus roll to the day of doom. They are idea boys and efficiency experts, who tolerate books only as long as there is no more efficient way for recording, preserving, and transmitting knowledge. They strayed into librarianship mostly from other fields, and they have never been at home since, for to them books in large numbers are merely a nuisance, and they spend their time trying to think up substitutes for them, jargonizing about automation, bibliographic control, contact points, mass media, decision-making processes, retrieval of information, and the dissemination of knowledge. They will do everything on earth to a book but read it.

At a conference on children's literature, criteria were examined for judging books, and when a librarian suggested that the best thing he could say about a certain book was that his little girl and her friends loved it, he was sent to the foot of the class. Personal response to a book is taboo, he was told; rather must it be judged by how well it integrates with the socio-directive pattern.

They are glib and they are patronizing, these modern enemies of books, and I intend to make war upon them in that they threaten the things I love. These lip servers are strongly entrenched and strategically placed, and if they prevail, the collections of books called libraries will be stored and deposited, cared for economically, it is true, but inaccessible and remote from scholars' and ordinary readers' eyes and hands. Gone will be the desire which animated Henry Stevens, John Carter Brown, or just plain John Carter; for without encouragement and guidance and example and immediate access to books, the bookish instinct becomes starved and dies. I am a practicing bookman today because I was *encouraged* to develop my basic bookishness, by my mother, my town librarian, two teachers at college, a printer and a bookseller, and finally by a city librarian.

I do not wish to be known as a biblio-mystic, and I am amused by Huxley's story of how Lawrence rejected modern science by putting his hands over his solar plexus and saying, "But I do not feel it down here"; and yet it is true that for me books are more than idea-husks. In northern New Mexico one summer I saw a boy lying in the grass beside his watermelon truck, where it was parked alongside an acequia, and he was reading something that can be held in the hand and carried in the pocket, not something just as good as or better than, but actually and simply a book, and with the same utter absorption that an English yeoman or itinerant preacher of three centuries ago might have derived from John Bunyan's handy little work on the Pilgrim's Progress.

Books are to be used as instruments in binding men closer in thoughtful good will, some with reverent care in that they are rare and precious and irreplaceable, others with a firm hand on their buckram backs, paper books with the same happy expendability with which Mother Nature regards the forest leaves, and always without snobbism or cultism, whether in reserve-book room or rare-book room, on the steps of a country bookmobile, or under the great dome of the British Museum or the Library of Congress. Read by sunlight, lamplight, or, as Lincoln did, by firelight, the book is still the best way man has found to record and transmit his knowledge. Machines can do much for us in controlling the flood of "firmed up but not finalized" near-print, off-print, or un-print material, but machines cannot communicate—at least not yet—by what Lester Asheim aptly calls "a kind of poetic shorthand."

This simple act of reading is universal, transcending time and place, so that sight of the Taos boy reading in the roadside grass made me think of another reader, old George Saintsbury, portrayed by Helen Waddell "in the Augustan twilight of the house of his last inhabiting, a solitary indomitable figure with straggling grey hair and black skull-cap, gaunt as Merlin and islanded in a fast-encroaching sea of books . . . reading, reading, reading through the small hours in the familiar chair with the two tall candlesticks behind it. And their light falls, not on his face, but on the open book."

I believe that books—those beautiful blends of form and spirit—have a future fully as glorious as their past; that to disbelieve this is an act of faithlessness, is dangerous, and could lead to the downfall of the kind of librarianship in which the book is central and basic. I know that I am not alone in my belief, my faith, my love, and I call on booklovers everywhere to close ranks, face the invaders, and give them the works, preferably in elephant folio.

That's how I feel about the bk.

THE MAGNETIC FIELD

BOOKISH PEOPLE will know what I mean by the title of this essay—that it is a figure borrowed from science, a phrase somewhat magical and poetical in itself, and which is intended to set up a sympathetic response in my readers, those who, like myself, are sensitive to books in their threefold aspect of material, intellectual, and spiritual being.

By *magnetic field* a scientist means that field of force around a magnet wherein a piece of iron, though not in contact with the magnet, will be attracted to it. Action-at-a-distance they call it. The concept of the natural magnet goes back centuries before the Christian Era, when the Greeks knew that the mineral lodestone, a magnetic oxide of iron, had the power to attract other pieces of iron.

Books also are magnets, with the power to attract people.

University of Tennessee library lecture, 1954.

THE MAGNETIC FIELD

A single book may have this magnetic force, and when hundreds and thousands of books are brought together in bookshops and libraries, their power is increased, so that such a place of bookish concentration possesses an irresistible attraction for readers and collectors.

Scientists will classify me as a sentimental fellow, shamelessly borrowing their terminology to lend his work a pseudomodern slant. And in his anger at my nerve the scientist might even borrow his terminology from Gertrude Stein to insist that a book is a book is a book, no more and no less than a man-made product of paper and ink, a mere lump of matter, mutely awaiting the passage of a man's eyes over its pages before it has any power of communication.

Now there may be scientists among my readers, but if so, they are pretty sure to be bookish as well, and it will be their biblio-antennae that are extended, and they will know that although my statement cannot be scientifically proved, it is none the less true that a book is one of the most powerful of all magnets, and that libraries and bookshops are places of power similar to the atomic piles wherein uranium is secretly split.

My essay is about some of my adventures in these magnetic fields of bookshops and libraries—the fields in which I have spent the best years of my life since I first learned to read and to love books more than any other creation of man's mind and hand. And though I could never prove to a scientist's satisfaction that a book is even more magnetic than the lodestone of iron oxide, I shall simply offer some examples of how this mechanism of flesh and blood and bone and something more, known as Librarian Powell, has responded to the magnetic power of books.

Three years ago I went on a book-hunting expedition to the British Isles. My chief weapon was a loaded checkbook. How to know what to aim at came from twenty years of experience in bookshops and libraries, plus knowledge of the resources and the needs of my own library at the University of California at Los Angeles. All of this was subjective knowledge that I carried in my head and drew upon with that invaluable bookman's tool, a memory (unfortunately not perfect) of thousands on thousands of books seen in the course of my travels and studies.

Science also was called upon to provide me with a piece of equipment to help in the location of unusually rare books. We have all heard of the geiger counter which reveals the presence of radioactive materials. I worked with one of our engineers, and with a surgeon in the medical school, in the fabrication of a biblio-geiger counter, a minute electronic device located by surgery in the epidermis of the little finger, and which in proximity to very rare books, pamphlets, and manuscripts begins delicately to tick and to tingle.

I had not been in London a month when the cost of this invention was far more than justified by the treasure it revealed. I was in a West End bookshop which dealt in very rare and expensive things, and although there was plenty to make my biblio-geiger counter function, the high prices kept the books out of my reach. I wandered around the shop, searching in vain for a bargain, and ended up in a basement room that served as a catchall. It was strewn with odd volumes, an orchard full of culls, and in a corner I saw a mound of pamphlets. The owner answered my inquiring look by saying that they were the dregs of a seventeenth-century collection that had come from a royal house in County Wiltshire. They had been creamed for rarities, he assured me, and what I saw was the skimmed whey.

I reached for a handful of the pamphlets, and jerked back my hand.

"What's the matter?" the dealer asked. "Did you see a spider?"

"Maybe it was," I said, reaching again and leafing through the pamphlets on the top of the mound.

What had happened was that my counter had jumped to maximum register and my heartbeat had matched it. I quickly turned off the counter and looked at something else.

"If you're interested in those pamphlets," the dealer said, "and will take the lot, they're yours for a dollar apiece. But if you insist on picking and choosing, they'll cost you two dollars apiece."

"How many are there?" I asked.

"Between two and three thousand," he replied.

"If I took the lot," I said, "duplication with what we have at home would run too high. Would you bundle them and let me work through them at home tonight? I'll probably keep several hundred."

The bookseller was agreeable, and so I took an enormous bundle home in a taxi with me to Chelsea, and spent most of the night hunting for the treasure that my tingler kept telling me was somewhere in the lot.

It was toward the gray of morning that I found it, and the reason that the dealer had missed it in his creaming of the lot was that it was a pamphlet smaller than the rest, and was stuck slightly to the one on top of it, so that in handling one, both were turned. What was it? It was a pamphlet by William Penn, our great Quaker pioneer, who in the latter part of the seventeenth century published anonymously *A Brief Essay on the Need for Peace in Europe by the Establishment of a Common Parliament*. It is an early plea for a United Nations, and in this particular edition of 1690 is so rare as to be known in only a single other copy, that in the Friends' Library in London. How much is it worth? Up to a thousand dollars.

I took my find back the next morning and paid the bookseller cash for it. Not the two dollars agreed upon, no; I demanded the customary library discount. William Penn's pamphlet cost the sovereign state of California one dollar and eighty cents.

While in England I also did some collecting for my personal library. Ever since college days I have collected and read the books of D. H. Lawrence, and my favorite of his novels is the last one he wrote, and which because of its frank language about love has never been legally allowed to be published in England and the United States.

Lady Chatterley's Lover was issued first by the author at Florence in 1928. I like the story of the Italian printer who set the book in type, not knowing a word of English. When he was warned that the book contained some naughty

English words, he asked what they were in Italian; and when he was told, he shrugged his shoulders, threw up his hands, and exclaimed, "But we do that every day!"

The first edition of *Lady Chatterley*, which consisted of one thousand numbered and signed copies on fine paper, is not too difficult to obtain, and costs about fifty dollars. The truly rare edition of the book is the second edition, also printed at Florence in 1928 and limited to only two hundred copies. Instead of fine paper, they were printed on cheap stock which did not stand up under the heavy reading that all copies of this book understandably get.

For years I looked in vain for a copy, and dealers kept trying to sell me a later and also cheap edition printed in Paris, and authorized by Lawrence to meet the pirating of the first edition. The booksellers insisted that this was the second edition, and that I must have dreamed up an intermediate edition, although Lawrence described it in his essay on *Lady Chatterley*.

Then in London during the fall of 1950 I entered the magnetic field of the book I was seeking. I was in the bookshop of a man whose former partner had been Lawrence's Florentine publisher, that legendary figure named Giuseppe Orioli who had died in Portugal during the war.

"I have some of his effects upstairs," his partner said. "Would you like to climb the stairs and see them?"

Up and up and up we went, and I knew when we entered the flat on the topmost floor that treasure was there, for my device was ticking away at top speed. Just what it was, I did not know at once. The dealer opened a desk drawer. It was packed with letters.

"From Norman," he said. "All written to Pino."

"Norman Douglas?" I asked, and looked at one or two of them. "For sale?"

"It might be arranged—to you" was the reply. "Do you want to examine them all?"

"There's no need to," I said. "Simply wrap and ship. I know they aren't too expensive."

"Of course not—to you."

They weren't.

They were not the treasure.

"Do you need a first of *Lady Chatterley?*" the dealer asked, looking toward a bookcase in the corner.

"No, thanks," I said, and almost went on to ask about the rare second edition. I caught myself and dropped to my knees in front of the corner bookshelves. Now my device was really going. I ran my hands over the backs of the books. The light was not good enough to read their titles. My fingers closed on a single paper-bound volume. I knew I had found it. Yes, it was the second edition of the "Lady."

I managed somehow to do two things I rarely do: to keep quiet and to wear a poker face. Then I pulled out several other volumes and took the lot downstairs, and asked the bookseller to price them. When he came to the Lawrence he sniffed.

"It's only a second edition," he said. "What do you want with it?"

"Oh, just an idea," I said, bending over to untie and retie my shoe. "I thought it would make a good lending copy instead of my precious first."

"In that case," the dealer said. "I'll throw it in free with the others."

And I let him do it.

Once a person enters the magnetic field of books and feels their pull he is lost for life, and he will want to spend all of his waking hours living with books, at work and at leisure, in libraries and bookshops, and to go to sleep at night with books beside his bed where he can turn to them in the still hours of sleeplessness, and begin each day with coffee and prose.

I think of my high school teacher of English from whom I first heard about Shakespeare. I was only fifteen then and a very naughty boy, a show-off and a tease, and I was assigned by her to a seat in the front row, right by her desk, where she could keep an eye (and sometimes a hand) on me.

That teacher loved books. Although more than thirty years have passed, I can remember the loving way she held a book and the passion with which she read from it.

Years went by and more vivid memories crowded out the one of this teacher, whose name was Miss Bear. Then a few years ago an incident occurred in my library which resulted in national publicity. A student attempted to steal the copy of the *Bay Psalm Book* which had been loaned to us for exhibit by Doctor Rosenbach. It is the first book printed in English colonial America, at Cambridge in 1640, and the last copy sold brought $151,000 at auction. We caught the thief and recovered the book—

thanks to God and the campus police—and a picture of me restoring the book to the exhibit case was flashed around the country by Wirephoto.

Soon thereafter I received a letter from Delta, Colorado, written by my old teacher, Ethel Bear, expressing satisfaction that I had at last become a solid and bookish citizen, and asking me to visit her if I ever passed through Delta.

I had to open my atlas to locate that Colorado town. It is about fifty miles upriver from where the Gunnison and the Colorado meet at Grand Junction, and is at a lesser river junction, the confluence of the Gunnison and the Uncompahgre. It did not seem likely that I would ever go through Delta. And then my rancher brother-in-law moved from Wyoming to Colorado, and took up a ranch on the Smith Fork of the Gunnison, about thirty miles above Delta.

We visited him one summer at this river ranch on the western slope of the Rockies, a peaceful place of timothy meadows, deep trout pools, and those fat ground hogs known as "whistle pigs." On the way back to Los Angeles I stopped in Delta and asked the way to the home of Miss Bear. It was a cottage on the main street, fronted by lawn and flanked by flowers and shrubs. No one answered the bell. Away on vacation, perhaps. I started back to the car, then quickly turned around and walked to the rear of the house.

There she was, a sturdy old lady picking roses. No mistaking Miss Bear; determination showed in everything she did, even picking roses. I walked up to her—probably a frightening sight in shirt by Sears and pants by Penney —looked her dead in the eye, Western style, and asked, "Do you remember me?"

She returned my look, same style, then backed off a bit, and her eyes were twinkling as she asked,

"Would you be that Lawrence Powell?"

I threw my arms around her and kissed both cheeks, delighted that she could still see the boy in the middle-aged man.

We went inside and she showed me her house and things. Every room had books in it, on shelves, tables, and even on the floor.

"I can't help it," she apologized. "They just come to me somehow. You know how it is, being a librarian. A *librarian!*" she said the word over again, and we both laughed at the thought that was in her mind, of her one-time bad boy having become ultrarespectable.

"Where did it all begin?" I asked.

"Right here in Delta," she replied. "When I was a little girl, in the public library—and I've loved books ever since, excessively, unreasonably, passionately, yes, and expensively. I should have been a librarian and gone around spending *other* people's money!"

"You're not lonely here, all by yourself?" I asked, knowing what her answer would be.

"Of course not! I have all the best people who ever lived for company. I was reading Emerson at breakfast . . . let me get it, I want to read it to you."

She trotted off to the kitchen and back, fitted her glasses, opened the book, and read; and magically time contracted and I was back in class again, a high school sophomore in the bad boy's seat, hearing Miss Bear read aloud. And this is what she read:

> We owe to books those general benefits which come from high intellectual action. Thus, I think, we often owe to them the perception of immortality. They impart sympathetic activity to the moral power. Go with mean people and you think life is mean. Then read Plutarch, and the world is a proud place, peopled with men of positive quality, with heroes and demigods standing around us who will not let us sleep.

I left Miss Bear among her books and roses, practicing to the end of her life what she had preached to her pupils, that next to mother's milk books are the best food.

I was in Phoenix, Arizona, not long after, having flown over from Los Angeles on a twofold mission, to visit the Indian sites in the Salt River Valley excavated in the 1880's by the first organized archaeological expedition to the Southwest, and to examine the collections on Southwestern literature in the State Library. Between the library visit and a dinner engagement I had a couple of free hours, and I went in search of a bookshop, a secondhand bookshop where I might find a few items on the want-list I carry in my head.

Phoenix is not distinguished for its antiquarian bookshops; in fact, it was a New Mexican who said that Phoenix is merely the desert trying to be like southern California: a lot of stuccoes and neons and not enough water. The university town of Tucson, a hundred miles to the south, is a better hunting ground.

I did find one old bookshop in Phoenix, however, a couple of miles east of the capitol, a barnlike place with a few naked light bulbs hanging on long cords, all but one of which were turned off. Two elderly men were seated at the rear of the store, one of them engaged in marking prices in a stack of books at his side, the other just sitting there watching him. Neither paid any attention to me.

"Mind if I put on a light?" I asked.

The bookmarker grunted, then said, "Go ahead, but as for me, I can find 'em better if it's not too bright."

And the other old gaffer piped up and said, "Those darned lights hurt my eyes too."

Was I dissuaded by this unusual kind of merchandising? No. Nothing dissuades a bookhunter, least of all bookseller resistance. I went about the dark shop, pulling on and off the dangling light chains, peering for the familiar and the unexpected. I found a Colorado River novel of a few years back, but which like many recent books has become scarcer than some a hundred years older. It is called *Crazy Weather*, by Charles L. McNichols, and is about a boy's adventures along the watercourse that forms the boundary between Arizona and California, a kind of Western Huck Finn.

In fact I found two copies, one marked one dollar, the other only fifty cents, and both were in good condition. I showed them to the bookseller and asked,

"How come the difference in price?"

He took both copies and studied them carefully. He took his hat off and put it back on. He blew his nose. Then he said,

"I see what you mean. At a dollar one's too high and at fifty cents one's too low. How about paying me seventy-five cents for a copy?"

The man interested me. Ignoring his odd way of doing business I looked closely at him while he went on marking books, then I asked,

"Were you ever in Los Angeles?"

"Yes," he replied. "And so were you."

"But it's my home," I said.

"I know you," he said. "Spotted you when you came in the door."

"You talk like a detective," I said.

"We get some suspicious characters in here" was his reply.

"Now I know you," I said. "You used to sell second-hand novels to the Los Angeles Public Library."

"Back in the Depression," he said. "When you were working for Albert Read in the order department."

"It was my first library job," I recalled. "And it was good old Albert Read who persuaded me to leave this bookselling racket and become an honest librarian. He was a wonderful little sparrow of a man!"

"Sparrow, hell! He was a vulture who fed on my profits!"

"He was only saving the city money," I said.

"Is he still doing it?"

"No," I said. "He retired ten years ago and went back into the trade, at Dawson's Book Shop. He couldn't keep away from books."

"Is he still there?" the old bookseller asked.

"No, he retired from Dawson's when he was seventy-five. That was five years ago. He died only last week."

The bookseller snorted and kept on marking the books in one pile and putting them in another.

"Read was a damn fool like the rest of us who haven't got sense enough to keep away from books. Take this shop, for example. I never wanted to buy it. Came over on a scouting trip once and this old so-and-so sold it to me. And now all he does is sit here on his tail and watch me do the work."

The older gaffer cackled at this and slapped his thigh. I took my fifty-cent purchase and departed on more urgent business. A magnetic field, yes, but of rather low power.

The bookstack in a great library is a place of high magnetic power. I had a demonstration of this several years ago on my first visit to Yale. Before leaving Los Angeles I called on one of Yale's oldest living graduates, Dr. Henry R. Wagner of the class of 1884, who retired at sixty from mining engineering and then became an increasingly distinguished historian and bibliographer, until then in his nineties, he was the Nestor of American bookmen. Wagner was a book collector from his college days.

"When you're in the Yale Library," he said to me, "be sure and see the collection on Irish economics that I gave them fifty years ago. Some bright young thing in the catalog department wanted to disperse the collection throughout the stacks by what was supposed to be the latest classification plan, but I raised so much hell that they kept it shelved intact. I want you to check up on them for me, will you, Larry?"

In the excitement of my first sight of the Sterling Library, I confess that I forgot about Wagner's charge. James Babb, the librarian, had been hiking me for miles through those Gothic acres of books, each succeeding sight of their treasures making me more covetous; and finally we took what Babb described as a short cut back to his office, which led us across one of the top levels of the stacks. Only the main corridor was lit, and all the side ranges stood dark.

Babb went on ahead and unlocked an exit door and waited for me to catch up. I started through the door, then I felt an irresistible urge to turn back several ranges and snap on the light switch. There I walked along the lighted range and looked at solid shelves of pamphlets, thousands upon thousands of them, all in uniform old bindings, really a noble sight of compressed power. Babb came back to see what had happened to me. He looked at the shelves, then exclaimed,

"How did you know the Wagner collection was here?"

"I didn't," I said. "I mean I guess I did! I told the old man I'd look for it. I'd forgotten about it until just now when something told me it was here."

Babb looked skeptical, as if to say that he knew someone must have directed me to this range.

"I'm completely lost," I said. "I didn't even know I was thinking about the Wagner collection when we cut through here."

THE MAGNETIC FIELD 37

"Well," Babb said, "you tell the old gentleman his collection is still the way he wants it."

Soon after arriving at Columbia University in the spring of 1954 to teach in the library school, I had a magnetic experience with a single volume, a work which is one of my favorite Southwest books. It is Mary Austin's *Land of Journeys' Ending,* and it contains memorable chapters about Arizona and New Mexico, and one in particular about the El Morro National Monument in New Mexico known as Inscription Rock. Upon this great buff-colored cliff of sandstone passing travelers, from the time of Don Juan de Oñate in 1605, have left their names inscribed in the rock, generally with the prefatory words *Pasó por aquí.*

A switchback trail leads to the top of the cliff whereon the Zuñi Indians once dwelled. Mary Austin loved this remote place, and although she knew that Federal law would prevent her from being buried there as she would have liked to be, she predicted that her ghost would at least haunt the Rock.

"You, of a hundred years from now," she wrote, "if when you visit the Rock, you see the cupped silken wings of the argemone burst and float apart when there is no wind; or if, when all around is still, a sudden stir in the short-leaved pines, or fresh eagle feathers blown upon the shrine, that will be I, making known in such fashion as I may the land's undying quality."

I climbed the Rock once in September, and although

I did not see Mary Austin's "ghost," I did sense most surely what she calls the "land's undying quality."

The startling experience came later in New York, when I dove into the Butler Library stacks and came up with Mary Austin's book in my hand. I charged it out, then carried it off, like a dog with a bone, to a far corner of the reading room, sat down and opened it. There, resting lightly on the title page, lay a blue feather, an actual bird's feather, that of a mountain bluebird, pristine and iridescent, making known to this reader that book's undying quality.

I was transfixed for a long moment, while the rustle of the reading room sounded softly. Then what did I do? The book was Columbia's, certainly, but just as surely, that feather was mine, placed there who knows when or by whom, awaiting a reader who would know what its meaning was. I was that knowing reader.

That was not the end of my strange experiences with Mary Austin. A year passed, after my return from Columbia to California, and then I was invited to speak to the Inyo County Teachers' Institute, meeting at Lone Pine in the Owens River Valley, the heart of Mary Austin's Land of Little Rain, lying at the eastern base of the Sierra Nevada. Here she had lived in the early years of this century as the young bride of the County Superintendent of Schools, put down roots in the then fertile valley, and drawn up the nourishment which resulted in her immortal book.

Then the city of Los Angeles, two hundred fifty miles away, decided its people needed the valley's water, took it away by aqueduct, and ruined the ranchers. Mary Austin fought in vain against this water rape, and in the end prophesied ruin for Los Angeles.

This was in my mind that night in Lone Pine when I stood before the teachers in the high school auditorium, and told them of Mary Austin's love for El Morro, of the blue feather in her book, and finally of her prophecy of ruin.

At that moment I paused and all was still. Then suddenly the side door of the auditorium rattled violently. The following silence was even deeper.

"Will someone open the door?" I asked, knowing well what would be seen.

One of the men teachers put his hand on the crash-bar and thrust the door wide open.

What was seen? Nothing at all. No one visible was there, or had been there.

Books are indeed strong magnets, packed with the power to attract people and to change their courses. These have been some of my experiences in the magnetic fields, testimonials of love for my favorite places on earth—bookshops and libraries.

THE POWER TO EVOKE

"THE POWER TO EVOKE." What does it mean? In choosing this title for an essay, I had in mind something quite personal; namely, that I find myself increasingly susceptible to the evocative power of handwriting, as compared to that of print. For me, autograph manuscripts possess a power to evoke their authors and their times, in a measure unmatched by that of any other form of communication. And it is in a personal, rather than a scholarly, manner that I shall write, with illustrations from my experience as a bookman.

As my life with books and manuscripts and their writers has widened and deepened, I have become increasingly watchful for and sensitive to signatures and annotations in books, to holograph letters and manuscript works, because of their power to summon images and memories,

A paper to The Manuscript Society, 1953.

THE POWER TO EVOKE 41

the ambiance of a time and a place. I am glad that the Association of Autograph Collectors has changed its name to The Manuscript Society. I must confess to a prejudice against autograph collectors. The term evokes for me the image of a foxy fellow snipping the signatures from letters and throwing the rest away. Or of bobby soxers, rushing a crooner into a corner, in order to get his signature in their albums. Or of myself as a boy, going with my father into the Chicago Cubs' dugout, accompanied by their owner, and emerging with an autographed baseball, signed by the entire team, including the famed Grover Cleveland Alexander.

For months that ball stayed immaculate. Then I tentatively played catch with it, albeit with clean hands and gloves, until finally I could stand it no longer, and the once precious sphere was batted into oblivion on the neighborhood sand lot. I have little patience with either collectors or libraries who look upon autograph manuscripts merely as museum pieces, to be stared at under glass, and not actively used for study and research. Not that I believe in wearing our manuscripts to shreds. Controlled use is what I mean.

That baseball was my first and only autograph signature collection. As one grows up, one puts away childish things —or should: cigar bands, bottle tops, match covers, stamps, and autograph signatures. I recognize a rising scale of values in collecting, from the primitive to the civilized, starting with shells and beads and culminating in manuscripts and books. And as a man himself becomes more civilized, he seeks more comprehensive and subtle manifestations of the creative impulse—books which reveal the vast range of human experience, and manuscripts which are the earlier flower, books being the fruit.

Manuscripts are to me the most basic, pristine, and vivid evidences of the creative spirit. Or let me say, for example, that a manuscript of a poem or play, an essay or novel or letter, is like the unclothed body of a man. All is revealed and made clear to the eye. The printed book, however, is the clothed man; often more attractive, it is true, but no longer completely revelatory and evocative.

I am not a graphologist, and yet I find myself fascinated by the infinite variations in human handwriting. I have a feeling of reverence before manuscripts. I loathe typescripts, except as a means of getting a manuscript translated into print. I see no point in preserving an author's uncorrected typescript, although I must confess to harboring more than one in my library, for want of better.

As for myself, I would no more think of composing any kind of writing directly on the typewriter, than I would of kissing a girl through plate glass. I cannot master our muscular and evasive English language, without forming the letters and the words and the sentences, with pencil on paper, directly shaping the language, as rivers write their signature on the land.

In the past twenty years I have handled manuscripts of many periods and languages, and always with delight in their variety and differences. I have sat drinking red wine with John Steinbeck and marveled at the prim way he penned the manuscript of his ribald *Tortilla Flat*, inscribed in his minuscular hand in blank ruled ledger books that had belonged to the Treasurer of Salinas County, California—his father.

I have worked every day for a month in a Los Angeles bank vault, cataloging the manuscripts of D. H. Lawrence. Most of them were written outdoors in a notebook held on his lap, and the Lawrentian script is as serenely regular as his books are not. I have had the thrill of discovering and transcribing the first manuscript newspaper on the Pacific Coast—the eccentric *Flumgudgeon Gazette and Bumble Bee Budget,* written in Oregon in 1845 by the Curltail Coon, a pseudonym subsequently revealed as that of the Virginia emigrant, Charles E. Pickett, better known as Philosopher Pickett.

I have traveled down the California coast, from Carmel to Big Sur, with a United States Topographic Survey map loaned me by the poet Robinson Jeffers; and when I turned it over and looked at the back I was amazed to find a maze of penciled manuscript notes, which I finally deciphered as the working draft of a narrative poem by Jeffers.

And I have handled hundreds of autograph letters and manuscripts of Oscar Wilde, all written rhythmically in one of the loveliest scripts ever penned, so characteristic of the wit and music and high style of the Irish master at his peak.

I am a great collector, reader, and lover of printed books, but believe that no creation of man has the evocative power of his holograph manuscripts. I want now to recall a few of these experiences with manuscripts, to try to recreate some of the excitement I have known in collecting and working with manuscripts. First let me unburden myself of something I've been carrying too long.

I am no calligrapher. I doubt that I am capable of mastering any careful hand. Certainly I am not patient. And when my little prose stream begins to flow, my cursive hand leans heavily to the right, and I have the devil of a time keeping up with it. And my secretary in deciphering it.

Besides who wants to have a uniform hand with a thousand others? If it is mere legibility that is sought, then one should use the typewriter. Which, I suppose, merely shows my ignorance of the aims of modern calligraphy. The joy of forming beautiful hand-written letters I can understand and approve—perhaps envy. The fact is I was conditioned early to hate calligraphers. It was in the Third Grade, or was it the Fifth? Her name was Miss Angevine and she came once a week to teach us arm-movement writing in the Spencerian mode. Remember? Those endless inky ovals! Those forests of push-pull, push-pull! "Lawrence, don't cramp your fingers so! Hold your pen loosely, and write with your whole arm from the elbow down!" I couldn't do it then, and I can't do it now. Since then I have written millions of words, with my fingers squeezing the lead out of a Scripto pencil; and I have yet to suffer the writer's cramp Miss Angevine threatened would be our fate if we didn't learn "arm movement."

Ah, but she smelled good though, when she came and leaned over me! I can forgive her everything now, for having smelled so sweetly of hair and skin, chalk dust, and newly sharpened cedarwood pencils.

THE POWER TO EVOKE 45

Now let us consider that English calligrapher who died in 1703. His name was Pepys—Samuel Pepys—and he was a great man in his age, the latter seventeenth century, the age of Dryden; and if he is the author of the raciest diary ever published, he was also Secretary of the Admiralty and "Father of the Royal Navy"; and as President of the Royal Society his name is the imprimatur on the title page of Newton's monumental *Principia*.

Highlight of my recent stay in England was the trip to Cambridge to see the library which Pepys left to his alma mater, Magdalene College; and the great moment of that visit was my first sight of the immortal Diary itself. Composed fastidiously in shorthand, each page's entry islanded in a sea of margins, the Diary manuscript puzzled me, disappointed me. It was *not* evocative of the popular Pepys. All the rich raciness of the Diary, its life-packed, swarming, sensual, indiscriminate abundance, was here reduced to a copperplate cypher. Did Pepys compose it pell-mell in longhand and later transcribe it into shorthand?

He kept it less than a decade and then, faced by blindness, he put it aside forever. It must have taken long nocturnal hours to compose, by candlelight, and it was guarded by him along with his moneybags, as his most precious possession.

Evocative or not of this or that aspect of Pepys's character, sight of the six quarto volumes of the Diary, running to three thousand and twelve pages in all, was one of the great manuscript experiences of my life. And that night, before going to sleep, I walked at twilight on the great green stretch in back of the University Arms Hotel known as Parker's Piece, and saw five simultaneous games of cricket being played. I was thankful for the fate that had spared Pepys's manuscripts from destruction. And so to bed.

Manuscript collectors might take as text a passage written by Pepys's friend John Evelyn. Certainly it was in my mind as I moved about Europe, hunting treasure with my trusty biblio-geiger counter. It reads:

> For it would grieve ones heart to make any farther Inquirie, were it not to stirr one up with the greater zeale to endeavor the finding out of such of them as may yet possibly lie hid and undiscovered, notwithstanding all the deligent searches which from time to time have been made. And therefore nothing ought to discourage the Learned and Curious, especialy such as amongst them are Travellars abroad, who have the greatest and most rightly advantages of any other, for the finding out these straid pieces, and reduce the scatter'd limbs of *Hippolytus*, as the most inestimable Treasure they can bring home, or oblige the world, and celebrate their names by to posterity: Nor are such to disdaine the rum'aging sometimes of the most neglected corners of Shops, and other obscure places, however cover'd with dust and cobwebs, wherever one may heare or suspect some old Parchments may have ben cast; and to enquire what Trades and other Crafts (besides the Leafe Gold beaters, Book-binders, past-boards, and the makers of Musical Instruments, who use it about the ribbs of Lutes, and other occasions) employ them in their works, and are us'd to buy, and have brought to them to sell, from Upholsters and Brokers, and from Country and

illiterate people and servants, who now and then light upon old and neglected *Manuscripts* cast behind the doore, or other blind corner of the house; and to procure amongst those sort of people that whatever old writings and parchments of that nature come to their hands, they be encourag'd to bring them to you, or give you notice; since by this meanes you may possibly happen upon that which may be a thousand times worth your paines and expense . . .

In following John Evelyn's advice I did a great deal of creeping through cobweb, of dodging the booby trap of dry rot, and of fighting frostbite with tea; and I made some rich hauls.

Probably the biggest strike of all was made by a purchase at auction. I am not one of those librarians who does his own bidding at auction. Here is where I lean heavily on my bookseller friends. When I saw a notice of a forthcoming sale of seventeenth- and eighteenth-century newsletters, partly printed and partly manuscripts—720 of them in all, dated from 1682 to 1710—I knew in a flash that I had to have them. And so I did something I rarely do—gave my agent absolute discretion to bid as high as necessary to get them for us.

This was in November of 1950. Before I could view the sale, I was called away from London on a trip to France; and on the actual day of the sale I was in Nice. I was at breakfast the next morning, savoring freshly baked *croissants*, sweet butter, and *café au lait* (the English may have the books, but the French have the food) when a cable was handed me. Just two words: GOT 'EM.

The following morning brought the *Times,* with an account of the sale and of the amount I owed my agent. It might have been worse. The collection of 720 letters cost only a little more than a dollar apiece. Yale and the Bodleian were the underbidders.

It was not until I returned to London and examined the bundle that I fully realized the richness of this haul. The letters were all sent by a London correspondent to a noble family in Derbyshire—a sort of Kiplinger news service it was—giving news and gossip in great abundance. The printed letters all included a blank page, on which the correspondent had added last-minute, stop-press news in manuscript.

I found them powerfully evocative of the London of Pepys's time. They also made me long (momentarily) for a life of retirement and seclusion, such as that lived three hundred years ago by another London diarist who was also a great collector and annotator of his books.

He was Narcissus Luttrell (1657-1732) who in the laconic words of the *Dictionary of National Biography,* "for many years lived in complete seclusion at Chelsea, studied much, chronicled the stirring events of his time, and collected an extensive library, including some valuable manuscripts."

His political diary was published a century ago, but a personal diary has never seen print. This latter is preserved in the British Museum, and I hopefully obtained a microfilm of it. What a disappointment! It was bad enough to find it written in Greek characters in the English language, but far worse to discover that it told hardly more than his hour of rising and who preached the day's sermon.

THE POWER TO EVOKE 49

More exciting is a bound volume in the Clark Library of poetical broadsides collected by Luttrell in the years 1683-84, and bearing the binder's title, "Poetry Long Waies."

On each broadside Luttrell wrote the date of the day he bought it and the price paid, together with sharp comments on the character of the pieces.

One of the great joys of collecting is the human fellowship it engenders. The best things are always happening to collectors. For example . . .

In a London dealer's catalog I saw listed a seventeenth-century indenture, bearing as one of the signatures that of John Dryden. At the Clark Library we are "crackers," as the English would say, about two authors, John Dryden and Oscar Wilde, of whose books and manuscripts we have unrivaled collections. We are now re-editing Dryden's complete works, for the first time since Sir Walter Scott's edition of 1808, and many a scrap is caught by our fine-toothed comb. My first thought in seeing the Dryden-signed indenture, was of vexation at the dealer's not having sent it to us with a bill, without even bothering to catalog it. Somehow she didn't—all of us have our lapses—and so I promptly cabled for it.

Vexation turned to something short of rage when the reply came back that the indenture had been sold. I ground my teeth and thought uncharitably of Huntington, of Yale, Harvard, Folger, Newberry, any one of which might have done this to Clark.

But no, it had been bought by an English writer, a Londoner who lived around the corner, figuratively speaking,

50   A PASSION FOR BOOKS

from the shop in New Bond Street. He was interested in Dryden, the wretch. And no, he would not give anyone a photostat. He was ill and cranky.

And so I settled back and waited for him to get better, or better yet, get worse—even die. He did. My eyes lit up one morning when I saw a four-line dispatch from London of this writer's demise. So sorry!

I cabled Miss Myers—why go on pretending to conceal her identity, the good Winnie Myers, the former Pooh-Bah of the Antiquarian Booksellers of America, great friend to manuscript collectors—and asked her to close in, not for "the kill," but for the post mortem.

More trouble.

The deceased writer's entire library of books and manuscripts, she reported, was to be sold at Sotheby's. Very well, I replied, bid in the indenture for Clark. Gladly, replied Miss Myers, but Professor Osborn of Yale wants me to do the same for him. He too had ordered the indenture from her catalog, and had later been rebuffed by the successful buyer.

Whereupon I sat down and wrote the following letter:

> Dear Jim: As you doubtless know, I have been after that Dryden document ever since Winnie Myers sold it to Meyerstein. Now I learn that it is coming up at Sotheby's on December 15. I am asking Miss Myers to bid for us. Are you determined to bid on this or would you be so kind as to yield to our pre-eminence in the Dryden field? I should be glad of course to give you a photostat, if we succeeded in getting the piece. It would seem to be most

unfortunate if our competitive bidding ran the price way up.

And received the following reply:

Dear Larry: Your letter about the Dryden document in the Meyerstein sale is welcome, and not unexpected. I shall be glad to withdraw my bid, of course, knowing that the document will find such an appropriate home.

The rest of this story is even nicer. It has to do with money. The indenture was originally sold by Myers for £18; and so at the Sotheby sale I gave them a top of £25. It was knocked down to us for £3/10!

Well known is the world-wide Walpole monopoly exercised by Wilmarth S. Lewis of Farmington, Connecticut—the fabulous "Lefty" Lewis, whose Yale Walpole edition is one of the noblest literary monuments of all time. Those who read the profile of him in *The New Yorker*, the pictorial spread on him in *Life*, and his own wise and witty book called *Collector's Progress*, know that Lewis has an undisputed claim on Walpoleana whenever it appears on the market. His magnetic charm has even extracted Walpole items from libraries which hitherto thought their treasures had come to stay.

All of this is common knowledge among bookmen. Less well known is the fact that "Lefty" Lewis, even as Jim Osborn, recognizes similar claims in other areas. Let me illustrate what I mean.

When Lewis visited the Clark Library last year he was impressed by the breadth and depth of our Oscar Wilde collection. It contains nearly four thousand items of print, manuscript, and picture, and I hope it will serve eventually as the basis for the first critical edition of Wilde's works, even as our Dryden collection is doing for the earlier century. When Lewis returned to Farmington he wrote me a letter, in which he confessed to having recently bought Oscar Wilde's seventy-five pages of unpublished manuscript notes for a lecture on Chatterton and Horace Walpole. He went on to say, "It is hard to determine the relative claims in such a case: Wilde versus Walpole-Chatterton, but I have tried to do so, and I think the Wilde interest of this manuscript is perhaps the greater. So—at the risk of appearing quixotically generous—I'll offer it to you for what I paid for it."

I mentioned earlier that I am not a graphologist or a handwriting psychologist. Yet I do believe that the study of handwriting and character is a vast terra incognita. Even when a man forsakes his natural hand for the anonymous Chancery script of the modern calligraphers, does that not tell us something of his character?

I often think of handwriting as a kind of musical symbolism, which begins to vibrate and sing and communicate only when the eye of man sets it free. No two natural hands are identical, any more than two men, even twins, are identical. What makes a man write as he does?

Last winter I visited Wilmarth Lewis at Farmington, and we talked about handwriting and character, with particular reference to Walpole. Nothing occurs at Farmington, even breakfast, without reference to Walpole.

THE POWER TO EVOKE

Later I asked Lewis to recall this conversation, and he wrote me as follows:

> In my opinion the study of handwriting is the most promising unexplored area left. Were I in your shoes I would build up as fine a library as I could on calligraphy. The significance of a man's handwriting as a key to his character and personality seems to me obvious. Unfortunately, it is a subject that is still not quite reputable. I told you how surprised I was when a great English historian (in a whisper) confessed that he employed a "psychographologist." Handwriting has been held in something the same repute as phrenology and reading tea leaves, but there is no question whatever in my mind of its immense value to scholars. I hope you will go briskly ahead and become the greatest library in the world on it.

Finally, I want to chronicle one more evocative story, of how a manuscript letter determined my vote in the 1952 presidential election. Up until summer I hadn't decided how I was going to vote. I was reared a rock-ribbed Republican by a father who was an associate of Mr. Hoover, and over my boyhood bed there hung a cherished picture, bearing the autographed inscription, "To Lawrence Powell from his friend Herbert Hoover."

And then Depression ruined my family and made a Democrat of me, after a brief and barren sojourn in the desert of the Far Left. The years passed, and by the summer of 1952, it was a tossup as to how I would vote. Although still a Democrat, I was skeptical of Adlai Stevenson, inclined to the suspicion that he might be the creation of an advertising agency.

Then I had lunch with Justin Turner, a few days before the Democratic convention, and he showed me a letter he had just received from Governor Stevenson. It was a holograph letter—a long letter, not a note—and it was *not* a solicitation of Turner's vote. It was not a political letter in any sense. It was rather a letter of thanks for a gift of Lincoln autograph material which Mr. Turner had made to the Illinois Historical Society. It was a wonderful letter, revealing a profound devotion to Lincoln, and it evoked for me all the pageant of American history—the Pilgrims and the rock-bound coast, the forest and prairie, the muddy rivers, mountains and desert, and the seacoast of California. And the men, ah, the men, the great Americans who are somehow always there when they are most needed, to rally us and to lead us, to speak for us in the tragic drama of history, and finally to go off-stage and yield their places to others.

All of this was both explicit and interlinear in Stevenson's hand-written letter, with an overpowering immediacy alien to the printed page.

I voted for Adlai Stevenson because of that manuscript letter. It spoke to me of sincerity, integrity, and culture, in the American tradition. And if he had to lose, I am glad it was to another great American who is our President now.

And that is what I mean by "the power to evoke."

THREE LOVES HAVE I

WHAT AM I DOING here in this beautiful stronghold of Clements and Adams talking about book-collecting? If ever a man carried coals to Newcastle—or should I say books to the British Museum?—it is I, invading one of the world's noblest libraries with the intention of talking about books, those helpless objects which are much better read than talked about.

The longer I live with books the more humble I become. There are so many of them, and although I have read thousands of books and handled even more and certainly looked at millions, I know that I will never satisfy a desire at least to look upon, if not read, every book ever written by man in all languages. For I love books with a passion that has never cooled, since my mother long ago handed

The Randolph G. Adams Memorial Lecture, given in the William L. Clements Library, University of Michigan, 1953.

me my first book, a now worn-out copy of *Grimms' Fairy Tales*. It is a vain desire, for my years are numbered and books are numberless.

My excuse for being here tonight is that I come with love in my heart and in my title. "What *are* these three loves?" I hear you ask. Speakers should get to the point. I shall, if you will be patient for a little longer. Am I not a librarian, and do not librarians do things in a systematic way? Thus far this is merely a prolegomenon to a title.

This seems to me the perfect time and the place to acknowledge my debt to the man whose memory we honor tonight: Randolph Greenfield Adams. At one time his was an almost lone voice in what he was convinced was the bookless wilderness of the American Library Association. And when I first entered the library world, in the summer of 1936, after a brief and educational career as the bibliofactotum in Jake Zeitlin's antiquarian bookshop, I too felt lonely. A year in library school made me lonelier, and when I was graduated in the spring of 1937 and no job was forthcoming, I reached the loneliest point of my life. All through library school I had been hopeful of landing a job that would pay me $200 a month. I had been supporting my wife and two children on less than half of that, and $200 a month would mean that we were secure for life. The best I could get was substitute work in the Los Angeles Public Library at $125 per month. While doing that—and it was valuable experience—I read an essay in a library periodical which was like a life preserver in a stormy sea or an oasis in the desert. It was Randolph Adams' classic "Librarians as Enemies of Books," a forceful and scholarly demand that librarians treat precious books with the decency they deserve. How it spoke to me, this voice for which I had been listening!

It was a year before I replied to it. In the meantime I had secured a grip on the bottom rung of the library ladder at UCLA and was hanging on for dear life, even climbing a little, when a break came. The head of the order department in which I was working asked me to suggest better ways of handling rare books the University Library had acquired in the Cowan Collection of Californiana. I had blown up when I caught an aid preparing to staple into a cardboard pamphlet-binder our copy of the California Constitution of 1849—a little item worth a thousand dollars.

The first thing I did was to write to Randolph Adams, asking for help. His reply was characteristic of the man. It was not by letter, telegram, or telephone. No. It was by the man himself in person. I was pecking away at my typewriter one morning, dreaming of what I would do if I ever became Head Librarian, when in came my friend and former employer, Jake Zeitlin, with a stranger in tow. It was obvious the man wasn't a Westerner, for he was carrying a hat.

"I'm Adams," he said, holding out his hand.

"Good Lord!" I said, as Jake grinned and nodded.

"Take me to your boss," Adams demanded. "I've got something to say to him."

Against my better judgment I escorted him to the inner sanctum of my predecessor, the late John E. Goodwin.

"I'm Randolph Adams," he said. "And I want you to

give Powell a free hand in looking after your rare books."

I fully expected to be summarily fired. Not only was I not fired, but I was actually given the hand Adams asked for. His forthrightness was irresistible. It was not until 1950, six years after I had succeeded Mr. Goodwin as University Librarian, that things were finally brought under so-called bibliographical control, with quarters available at last for the care and use of rare books and other irreplaceable library materials. I wanted Adams to speak at the dedication; by then however he was too ill to travel. Our Department of Special Collections is a small monument to the man's rare qualities of inspiration and purposeful energy.

That was the beginning of a friendship which lasted as long as Randolph Adams lived. Alas, I never visited him here. The nearest I came was in the winter of 1950. Fog grounded my Detroit flight at La Guardia Field, and before I could make another trip east, my chance was lost forever to see the man in his perfect environment.

He was wise, he was forthright and courageous, and he was kind; and he knew and loved books as few among us do. I feel him at my side now and always and in all that I do, as if he were saying to me and to all bookmen, "I will go with thee, and be thy guide, in thy most need to go by thy side." And I speak tonight as one of this guiding man's loyal and grateful disciples.

I have now arrived at my title. Any good bookman would know that the reference is to books, and not to women, wine, and song. The three loves I have are:

Collecting books
Keeping books (which includes reading them)
Giving books away

The instinct to collect is a primitive one. Cavemen collected shells, savages gather beads, children hoard bottle tops, match covers, and marbles. The collecting instinct reaches its apotheosis in books. No other product of man is so much man himself. As a work of art a book, such as the Nash Dante, can delight the eye by its beauty of binding, of paper, and type. By its contents it can shake the heart as Shakespeare does, uplift the mind as Plato's *Dialogues* do, or make you laugh even as it removes your head—think of *Candide* or *Gulliver*.

The book can be all things to all men of all times, and there is no substitute for it. Films? Slides? Television? These so-called audio-visual aids are camp followers of the book, and lame ones at that. Don't let anyone sell you something "just as good" as a book. These other so-called media complement the book but they do not replace it. Throughout its five-hundred-year history, the book has acquired great symbolical power.

Imagine a collection of audio-visual aids in a building such as this! The basic book-collections of the world's great libraries—the British Museum, the Library of Congress, Yale University, for example—were formed by the refined collecting instinct of individual men. A good small nuclear collection of books in a library often proves strongly magnetic. Like attracts like. Most of the country's great libraries grew from such nuclear beginnings.

The collecting instinct should never be discouraged in

children. It will evolve as the individual evolves. Let me tell a family story. Most of us have collected juvenile series when we were kids. Remember the Rover Boys, the Dave Porter series, the Henty and the Altsheler books? When he was a boy, our elder son collected volume after volume of what I regarded as an extremely decadent boys' series called the Dave Dawson books. When my wife and I went abroad three years ago and left our boys in boarding schools, we stored their books in the garage. Only last week did we get them out, unpacking and sorting certain books for various charitable destinations. The Dave Dawson series we dismissed as out-of-date World War II stuff, and put the dozen volumes in a pile for the Salvation Army.

Little did we reckon with our twenty-year-old son, rough and tough from working all summer for the Municipal Department of Water and Power. He came home tired from a day's work in the desert heat of the San Fernando Valley, but when he saw the stacks of books his face lit up. "My Dave Dawsons!" he cried, falling on his knees beside them. "I wondered where they'd gone!" And he began to pore through them, as the joys of boyhood reading returned in flood.

"We thought you'd outgrown them," my wife said, in her most tactful manner, "and that we'd give them to the poor children."

"Poor children, my eye!" our son cried. "These are my books and I'm going to keep them forever."

I hope he does, but I'm afraid he won't. Collecting books is easy fun; keeping books, in face of today's forces of disintegration, is hard work. By the way, whatever happened to *my* Rover Boys?

Libraries are obviously no place to experience the joyful excitement of book-collecting. It is a penal offense to collect books from libraries with the intention of keeping them, and if I had my way, it would be a capital offense. Bookshops are different. They exist solely for the collector. In fact they can't survive if collectors don't take away their books and leave money in their place.

I have been in many of the world's great bookshops, collecting for the University of California, and have removed thousands of books, leaving dollars in their stead. I have hunted books on the main floor and on the mezzanine, up in the attic and down in the cellar. I have crawled on dusty floors and climbed up shaky ladders. I have paid too much for some books, too little for others. I have worked in overheated American shops and underheated British ones, oblivious to both heat and cold. I have competed with pigs and chickens in one shop. The joy that I experience in bookshops has nothing to do with their size. I like them all.

I was in a small one last summer in the upland village of Taos, New Mexico, at the foot of the Sangre de Cristo Mountains, and although it did not have many books or any rare ones, it did have a good selection of new books and a few antiquarian volumes of regional interest—D. H. Lawrence, for example, Taos being near the ranch whereon his remains are enshrined.

It was a Sunday afternoon in September, under a cloud-flocked cobalt sky, and I was glad to take sanctuary in the bookshop from the traffic-crowded narrow streets, most of the motorists being Texans, fugitive themselves from too much Texas. I bought only half a dozen paperbound books, but they pleased me much when later I retrieved the parcel from a roadside cache, where I had concealed it while I walked the dusty way to the Indian pueblo and back, then carried it to a cool room in the shade of great cottonwoods, and performed that immemorial rite of the book collector—lovingly untied the little package and pored through its contents.

It was a book of colored photographs of Paris that most stirred my imagination. Sight of such fabulous places as the Furstenberg Square where Delacroix had his studio, and of the Place des Vosges where Victor Hugo lived, and of Sacré Coeur from whose white steps I once saw sunrise over Paris—these moved my memory, and not just my visual memory, but the olfactory as well, so that there in the northern reaches of New Mexico, far from the river-souled city of light, I had only to close my eyes and straightway the room was permeated with that characteristic perfume of Paris—a bittersweet blend of coal smoke and Chanel.

Ah, this smell that different cities have! Shanghai's of sandalwood and excrement. London's of wet stone and dry books. Roasting coffee in San Francisco. Acrid smog in my home town, the Queen of the Angels. And in Taos and Santa Fe, the fragrance of piñon smoke.

This total stimulation of book-collecting is what makes

it such an irresistible passion. The hunting of books in every kind of shop or in dealers' catalogs, the capture and the carrying them away to one's den where the prize can be inspected in privacy, and then the overtones that follow reading—there is no magic like it, no enchantment on earth as fatal.

There is a difference between what I collect institutionally and what I collect privately. At UCLA, for example, we are collecting everything printed in Southern California since 1900, and I mean everything—books, pamphlets, maps, leaflets, broadsides, menus, tickets, etc. Our collection now numbers about 10,000 items, a fascinating potpourri, in which if one looks hard he may discern some kind of social evolution.

My own collecting of Southern Californiana, however, is confined to a single type of book: novels which are laid in and around Los Angeles. There are hundreds of them, for my home town does things to writers—provokes violent emotions in them, so that the novels about Los Angeles are a lively lot. I compiled a selective bibliography of them which I called *Land of Fiction* and chose therein about three dozen as being the cream of the crop, ranging from *Ramona* in 1884 to *The Loved One* in 1948. I have yet to assemble personally a complete collection of these three dozen books, for many of them are almost impossible to locate outside of public libraries. I had to go all the way to London, for example, to find a copy of *Merton of the Movies,* which I rank as the best of all novels about the movies.

In my own private collection there is neither rhyme nor

reason in my taste or in my method. In addition to Los Angeles novels, I collect the Greek Anthology and Chinese poetry in English, books about the *Titanic* disaster and books about fountains, and the works of individual authors from Shakespeare to D. H. Lawrence. I once had the best John Steinbeck collection in the country, up through his *Grapes of Wrath,* at which time he fell into a slump of success and produced a series of books that could have been written by any popular novelist. My collection went to Harvard.

Now when I no longer want to read and reread my books, I give them away, rather than sell them. This third love of mine—giving away books—can be as much fun as collecting and keeping and reading them, and, who knows, may prove a better passport to heaven.

The selfish pleasure of giving away one's books, when it is done on the grand scale by those who have both good taste and much money, results in libraries such as the Clements, the Clark, the Morgan, the Folger, Carter Brown, the Chapin, and the Huntington, as well as the Astor-Tilden-Lenox nucleus of the New York Public Library. If a recipient of rare books does not know what to do with them, they are indeed a problem. In 1938 I found them so, when my desire to do something about properly handling rare books in a university library exceeded my knowledge of what to do. I compiled a primer called "The Problem of Rare Books in the College and University Library," followed by an article with a poor title, "The Function of Rare Books."

Still later I published some rules of thumb for determining whether or not a book is rare and valuable, and when the Associated Press picked this story up from the University's clipsheet, I received many offers of supposed rarities. A correspondent in eastern California—I mean Iowa—sent me the torn-out title page from a 1905 edition of *The Pilgrim's Progress,* saying that if the item were valuable, he would forward the rest of the book.

Now it is all right, I say, for a beginning librarian such as I was fifteen years ago, to be confused about rare books, but when the librarian of one of the country's greatest libraries, which has yet to establish a rare-book room, confesses that he too finds rare books a problem and has only tentative plans to care for them, then am I reminded of the conclusion to "Librarians as Enemies of Books":

> ... the librarian who has become an impersonal administrator has disqualified himself for exercising some of the most important functions of his job. Someone else will have to take on these functions, and it ought to be part of the training of every librarian to see that someone else is equipped to do this work. Book collecting and the building-up of great libraries is as much a matter of the heart as a matter of the head. The man who is all heart and no head would be a very bad librarian. But the man who is all head and no heart is a very dangerous librarian.

I have spoken of giving away books in the grand style, a pleasure most of us can never know. I must say that I do not share the pessimistic view that the age of great private libraries is over. The passion to collect books cannot be cooled even by high taxes. I certainly find such taxes obnoxious, but I am not led thereby to ignore the fact that they can be a potent inducement to library donors.

Tax deduction has not been my motive however in the gradual transfer of my own books to the library of my alma mater—that of Occidental College in Los Angeles. The books I have collected since childhood have never been worth much money. I have given them away, a few hundred a year, with the hope that they would find other readers to whom they would speak as they have spoken to me, in times of plenty, in times of need.

My hope was realized last summer when in a Pasadena department store I chanced to encounter a recent Occidental College graduate.

"I have been wanting to meet you," he said, "to tell you that all through my college course I was always coming across some odd book or other in the library that bore your gift plate."

"What do you mean by 'odd' book?" I asked.

The young man looked embarrassed. "I guess I mean 'unusual.'"

"I know what you mean," I assured him.

"I guess we've got the same queer tastes," he said, then quickly added, "I mean unusual!"

And I recalled an experience I had last spring in the University of Arizona Library. It was my first visit to our neighbor in Tucson, and as I always do when I am in a library, I spot-checked the card catalog for a few of my favorite books.

Arizona did not fail me, and in three cases the catalog card bore the same symbol: "Hanley Collection." I didn't have to be told what this meant. The books were part of the 30,000 volumes T. E. Hanley of Bradford, Pennsylvania, has given to Arizona over the past fifteen years. What good taste the man has! was my thought, and when I returned to Los Angeles, I wrote Ed Hanley (whom I had last seen twenty years ago when I was working in the antiquarian bookshop) of my appreciation of what he was doing for a Southwest library, and received this reply:

"Thanks so very much for your most unexpected and kindly letter. It gave me a tremendous lift and I am deeply grateful."

It is not necessary to give thousands of books or a grand building, to be an Ed Hanley or a Will Clements. A single good book contains the fruit of the past, the flower of the present, and the seeds of the future. Whether it sags in shabby binding, one among millions in a university library, or, bound by Bedford, shines in sumptuous quarters such as these, or finger-smudged and food-smeared with its filthy fellows fills a few short shelves in a small-town library, a book is a unique and precious thing, and nothing on earth can supplant it as a source of power and of beauty.

Though not ordinarily an occult person given to dreams and visions, I am never in a library that I do not feel unseen presences around me, the ghosts of authors come back to see if their books are being read; of angry donors in search of the vandals who perforated the title pages of their Baskervilles; or of just plain readers who want no other heaven than a library. Last year in the Alderman Library at Virginia I sat reading one rainy evening, with students and staff swarming around, and I felt the undying vitality of the University's great founding bookman—Thomas Jefferson.

The year before last in the Bodleian Library I likewise felt the presence of old Benlowes, the seventeenth-century poet whose *Theophila* is physically the most beautiful book of his century. During youth and manhood Edward Benlowes was rich and gay, handsome and generous—the perfect Cavalier, whose pseudonym was Benevolus—but in old age he lost everything but a pittance. In his poverty he retired to Oxford where he spent the daylight hours reading and writing poetry in the Bodleian Library, from which no books could be withdrawn. Second only to the Vatican in bookish fame, the Bodleian boasted a staff of four—the librarian, his deputy, his assistant, and the janitor. Heat it had not. Muffled up in winter clothes, old Hyde the librarian cataloged the books, boasting with frosty breath of his immunity from the cold.

In spite of the cold, books and poetry continued to be Benlowes's delight until the end of his life, to an extent that caused the university bigwigs to marvel at his simplicity and unworldliness. Poetry stuck to him as closely as his poverty, said Doctor Fell of Christ Church. The winter of 1676, however, proved too much for the old poet. According to Anthony à Wood, it was the bitterest winter in memory, all rimy and misty, when the rivers froze and the people built huts on the ice. Fish and fowl perished in large numbers and "for want of conveniences required fit for old age, as clothes, fuel and warm food to refresh the body, old Benlowes died at eight in the evening on the 18th of December, aged 73 years or more, and was buried with academic honors in St. Mary's Church, under the north wall, his head near to the entrance of the vestry where the doctors put on their robes."

Browning has a poem called "De Gustibus," which begins "Your ghost will walk, you lover of trees, if our loves remain, in an English lane by a cornfield side aflutter with poppies." This might be altered to read, "Your ghost will walk, you lover of books, if our loves remain, in the Bodleian or the Clements, through the book-rich rooms and silent stacks."

I cannot conceive of Randolph Adams' spirit as ever being anywhere but here, now and forever, the blessed spirit of a good bookman come to his rest. We are his successors, and we will be succeeded by others. May we hand them as sharp a sword as we received from him, to be used with as much vigor upon the enemies of books, wherever they raise their heads!

IN IT TOGETHER

Booksellers and librarians have much in common, and I have observed that of the two, booksellers are the more aware of this. Librarians sometimes suffer from a withdrawal complex. They fail to recognize the economic base which underlies the writing, publishing, selling, and collecting of books. This shrinking kind of librarian would like to know the bookseller only *in absentia*—by catalog, by telephone, or letter, and to have him silently slip orders into the shipping room and as silently slip away.

I believe that librarians and booksellers should have the fullest knowledge and understanding of their common interests, should come and go freely in one another's libraries and shops; that they should illuminate dark areas of mutual misunderstanding, and work together in the

First published in the Antiquarian Bookman, *July 9, 1949.*

common good, which is that more and better books are sold and bought and read.

I welcome this opportunity to write about some of the advantages of a good working relationship between bookseller and librarian, to observe some things librarians can learn from booksellers, and ways in which dealers can profit from the experience of librarians, and finally to suggest means by which both can work together in their community to raise the level of culture.

One of the most important things a librarian can learn from a bookseller is to be ever aware of the intellectual and material value of books. Too often the librarian sinks into a stupor of routine, in which he goes through the motions of checking books in and out with an eye only for their call numbers. Too busy to read is the cry of this robot librarian, and to my ears it is a death cry. God help him who is too busy to read, for he has forfeited his claim to professional rank.

The best booksellers I have known have been readers of their stock. Bibliophile customers like to be served by dealers who have looked beyond the backs of books. A bookseller need not be a profound student or a specialized scholar. His knowledge of books should be wide and flexible. If a dealer does not have such familiarity with his stock and with books at large, he will neglect fruitful areas in which to sell and to buy.

Another thing the librarian can learn from the dealer is respect for that person without whom the dealer's stock would shrivel and his purse shrink. I mean the private book collector. Booksellers need no lecture on the importance of him who is their books and butter. Not so with librarians. Many biblio-technicians and library educators fail to envision the cycle which leads books from publisher to the open market, thence to the bookseller and into the hands of the private, specialty collector, from where they often go en bloc to libraries, either by dealer-arranged sale or by gift.

This country's distinguished libraries—the Huntington, the Morgan, the Brown, Clements, Wrenn, Chapin, Clark, Bancroft, for example—are monuments to the collectors who formed them, and in many cases to the booksellers who did the searching, the reporting, the buying, and the selling. Great libraries are often the result of two men's heroic labor. This is also true of the special collections which make university libraries outstanding.

It is obvious that a private collector, immersed in business or philanthropy, is wise to entrust his collecting to a trustworthy and knowledgeable dealer as, for example, Coe did with Eberstadt, Huntington with Smith, and Clark with Rosenbach. It is not true however that a large library, with perhaps several hundred thousand dollars a year to spend in several dozen fields of knowledge, can profitably place its buying in the hands of one or two dealers. No bookseller could ever cover such a fiscal and intellectual front. Nor can a library wisely acquire books and sets without competitive pricing.

This does not mean that a librarian should wear out himself (and the dealers' patience) by endless shopping around or by senseless haggling. When one finds librarians

IN IT TOGETHER

doing this, he may be pretty sure that they are covering up their own ignorance of books and values.

It is an unforgettable experience to watch a good bookbuyer—either dealer or librarian—at work on a roomful of raw material. Who can ever forget the late Ernest Dawson in the act of appraising a lot of books? With eyes and hands, and certainly a sixth sense, he sorted the plums from the culls, using reference books when in doubt, fencing nimbly with an owner on a disputed valuation, giving as well as taking—a Toscanini of the tomes.

There has probably never been a great bookseller who was not also a great bookbuyer. If and when I have the opportunity of planning a library school curriculum, I shall require a course in the buying and selling of books, on the economics and the diplomacy of book-collecting, shaped around the trinity of book collector, bookseller, and librarian.

I have yet to meet a bookseller whose shop has a history of a year or more, who was unaware of the economic base of bookselling. There *must* be a margin of profit. No fool can flourish long in the booktrade. The bookseller must compete for the collector's and the librarian's dollar, and the best collectors and librarians are those who can get the most and best books for their dollars.

When the critics of F.D.R. wanted to rout a defender of the President, their final argument was to the effect that "that man" couldn't possibly be worth anything because he had never had to meet a payroll. I know this is the way some booksellers feel about librarians, particularly those librarians who are slow in certifying dealers' bills for payment. It would do every order librarian good if he could interne a while in a bookstore, particularly at the bookkeeper's desk.

If they want to keep their trade credit good, booksellers must pay *their* bills regularly and promptly. The history of bookselling is strewn with the wrecks of those who failed to heed this universal law. Librarians should recognize this fiscal fact and pay booksellers as promptly as they can. This means that a good librarian will have friendly and persuasive relations with his institution's accounting department and know how to expedite payment when a dealer calls for help.

It has been my experience that librarians have more to learn from booksellers than vice versa. My own apprenticeship in the booktrade was every bit as valuable a preparation for librarianship as was the graduate year I spent in studying for a professional degree. In every aspect of my library work I have benefited from the knowledge of books and people which I derived from working in the booktrade. In fact, my education still goes on, as on my travels I observe booksellers at work. On trips to New York my time is usually divided between bookshops and libraries. Only once was I foolish enough to go to a musical comedy. Halfway through the production—which I found neither musical nor comic—I came to my senses and asked myself, What am I wasting my time here for, when New York is stacked with millions of books for sale? I rushed out of the theater and made a "bookline" for the shops of Fourth Avenue.

Take the average bookshop and the average library and

I find the former the more stimulating place to visit and to browse in. One meets more varied and interesting people in bookshops, and often the librarians one has the most in common with. There is something frustrating about encountering desirable books in libraries other than your own. This is not true in bookshops. In a library one can only flirt with the books he meets. In a bookshop one can encounter and possess.

Librarians have much to gain from meeting booksellers on the latters' own grounds; but it is also true that dealers can learn a few things from librarians. I will venture to enumerate them.

First, librarians are more orderly housekeepers than are booksellers. Dealers can learn the virtues of system and classification by studying library methods. Many bookshops are unpleasant to buy from because they are illogically arranged, poorly lighted, badly cleaned. Not enough imagination goes into the physical arrangement of most antiquarian bookshops. A veteran book buyer does not want to encounter "atmosphere"; he wants to have books visible and accessible; and he wants to see different books whenever he visits a bookshop. Nothing repels him more than static stock. If a dealer is unable continually to turn over his stock, he ought to become a librarian.

Booksellers who depend on catalogs and lists to sell their books can learn much from librarians on arrangement and format. I receive from six to a dozen booksellers' lists and catalogs every day. Most of them I open at once, and glance through quickly in search of certain types and titles of desiderata which are always nesting in my head.

Some I route to staff members and faculty; the rest I take home at night and check after dinner when the house is quiet. Many lists and catalogs are too hard to check because of crowded or faulty printing or mimeographing, or unclassified arrangement. I will rarely go clear through a straight alphabetical arrangement of hundreds of titles. I am not omniscient. Only in certain categories of printed books am I competent to select items for a university library; and thus classified catalogs are what I thrive on. Poorly mimeographed lists I discard after the first glance.

Another thing dealers can learn from librarians is accuracy in describing an item. I have lost patience with booksellers who consistently fail to give exact descriptions of the books they catalog—and they have lost my custom. I like Roy Vernon Sowers' emphatic frankness about condition in the foreword to one of his catalogs:

> In view of my own experiences recently in buying from catalogs, here and abroad, I wish to emphasize that my descriptions of condition are accurate. I consider fine condition an important factor in the price of a book or a print and I do not use that term loosely. I do not like the current use to cover a multitude of sins of that meaningless phrase "mostly good to fine"; and I am sorry to see the gradual elimination from English catalogs of accurate description of condition. There it is the natural result of years of war and bombings and wholesale damage; but there is certainly no reason for us in America to forget the distinctions between dingy and good and nice and fine and mint copies.

IN IT TOGETHER

The chapter on "Condition" in John Carter's *Taste and Technique in Book-Collecting* should be committed to memory by every bookseller and librarian—along with the rest of that excellent book.

A good bookseller will study the library collections in his region and buy materials with them in mind. No sales effort is required to sell journal gaps to a library, and every library has certain specialities in which it will buy fairly priced desiderata without hesitation. And yet many antiquarian dealers go on buying and trying to sell in the dark. Sharpshooting will bring down more library dollars than shotgun blasts.

There is a third and last thing which booksellers can learn from librarians: that is to establish a recruitment and apprenticeship program which will insure the trade getting a constant supply of young blood, in keeping it, and being succeeded by it.

Bookselling is an ancient and honorable trade, but to my knowledge little effort is being made to interest high school and college graduates to engage in it. Too many booksellers traffic in slave labor. It is true that beginners are economic parasites until they can daily sell their weight in books, but I believe that it would pay dividends if a bookseller would offer a subsidized apprenticeship to promising recruits.

What can booksellers and librarians do jointly to raise the cultural level? They can find common grounds on which to meet and to work together. I have in mind book fairs and forums, jointly sponsored exhibitions, mutual campaigns against censorship of books whether in shops or libraries, joint action against discriminatory postal rates on books, professional societies in which they can jointly hold membership.

Booksellers and librarians are brothers in the book. In the beginning was the spoken Word, then the written, and since Babylon, Alexandria, and Gutenberg's Mainz, men have sold clay tablets, papyrus rolls, and printed books, while other men have bought and read them, and, moved by love and pride, collected great libraries. Three hundred years ago Milton proclaimed that books are not dead things, and since then our people have had the freedom to write, to sell, and to read books more pregnant with life, more immortal than any man. Booksellers and librarians trade in immortal merchandise. They are in it together, and there is one name for them both. I pen it with pride. The name is Bookman. Long may they flourish!

EUCALYPTUS TREES AND LOST MANUSCRIPTS

IT IS MY IMPRESSION that most Californians like eucalyptus trees. True, they are a bit messy when it comes to raking up their litter, but no tree is more beautiful in the wind or against the sky, and none provides better nesting for the soft-voiced mourning dove. As for firewood, the bittersweet smell of this wood is evidence of a nonsparking blaze almost as slow burning as oak.

But this is not a treatise on the hundred-odd varieties of the tree which Australia sent to California in the 1860's and which has since become as symbolic of the Golden State as the orange and the geranium. It is my intention rather to tell how the eucalyptus tree was instrumental in bringing to the UCLA Library two of the most significant modern manuscripts ever to be added to the mushrooming collections on the Westwood campus.

First published in the California Librarian, *January 1956.*

I was at Mills College in Oakland to give the annual lecture on book-collecting which precedes the Hattie Sloss awards to the best student collections. No other campus in the state has such beautiful groves of eucalyptus, for they were planted nearly a century ago and have a long headstart on such upstart campuses as Occidental (1914) and Scripps (1927). Along with service-club luncheon groups, college students can be the best of all audiences, once their initial attention is captured; otherwise it's like shoveling smoke into the wind to hold their interest.

On the Mills campus, I found myself in need of something to open my talk, which would take the young ladies' minds off what all normal young ladies have their minds on at that particular time of year, which was spring, and which is not books; and so I thought of the diatribe on the eucalyptus tree written by Norman Douglas, the Scottish author whose satirical novel *South Wind* won him wide fame upon its publication in 1917. This passage occurs in his almost equally famous travel book *Old Calabria,* an account of the toe of the Italian boot, and is indexed as "Eucalyptus trees, a scandalous growth." Read what this otherwise discerning Scot had to say about our favorite tree:

> A single eucalyptus will ruin the fairest landscape. No plant on earth rustles in such a horribly metallic fashion when the wind blows through those everlasting withered branches; the noise chills one to the marrow; it is like the sibilant chattering of ghosts. Its oil is called "medicinal" only because it happens to smell rather nasty; it is worthless as timber, objectionable in form and hue—objection-

EUCALYPTUS TREES AND LOST MANUSCRIPTS 81

able, above all things, in its perverse, anti-human habits. What other tree would have the effrontery to turn the sharp edges of its leaves—as if these were not narrow enough already!—towards the sun, so as to be sure of giving at all hours of the day the minimum of shade and maximum of discomfort to mankind?

I entered the college library just before my lecture and called for *Old Calabria*, so that I could quote this libel as a curtain raiser. Alas, the library lacked a copy, and I told the students instead that the first thing I was going to do on my return home was to send one of my three copies of *Old Calabria* as a gift to Mills College.

So I went to my shelves back home that night and tried to decide which copy I could best do without. Not the valuable first edition, published in 1915, for all that was needed by the college students was a reading copy. Not the little World's Classics reprint, worth only a dollar, but of sentimental value to me because I had read it on my brief lunch hours during the war when I had held a laborer's job in a defense plant in Vernon.

That left another reprint, also of sentimental value, because it had belonged to A. Gaylord Beaman, prominent Los Angeles insurance man whose library had been bought and sold by Dawson's Book Shop after Beaman's death in 1945. I took this copy down and leafed through it. Something fluttered to the floor. It was a page torn from a bookseller's catalog, offering three original manuscripts of books by Norman Douglas: *Fountains in the Sand*, a travel book about Tunisia, *Alone*, an account of a walking trip in northern Italy, and *Old Calabria* itself. All three were priced reasonably enough, and after sending the book off to Mills, minus the insert, I sat down and wrote to the bookseller to ask who had purchased the manuscripts. I had in mind requesting permission to make microfilm copies for the Norman Douglas collection at UCLA—a collection founded on a bequest of first editions from Leon Gelber, late San Francisco bookseller, and which includes such odd titles as *On the Herpetology of the Grand Duchy of Baden* and *Report on the Pumice Stone Industry of the Lipari Islands*.

At least a dozen years had passed since Beaman tore out that catalog page and tucked it away in his book, and it might well prove that the manuscripts had long since been sold and no records kept. But no. Back came a letter from the dealer, that two of the three manuscripts were still available, stowed away and forgotten on a closet shelf, and if we would buy both of them, the two might be had for the original price of one. My affirmative reply went by telegraph.

Written in ink on foolscap in Douglas's tidy hand, the manuscripts of *Alone* and *Fountains in the Sand* were both bound in boards, covered with Florentine flowered paper, evidence of his long residence in the Tuscan town.

The Tunisian manuscript was heavily rewritten interlinear, but in order to keep head above the flood of research materials pouring every day into the library from all over the world, I could only glance at the Douglas items before turning them over to Wilbur Jordan Smith, head of the Department of Special Collections, with the suggestion that he show them to John Espey, the writer who teaches English at UCLA and who is contemplating a biography of Norman Douglas.

It was Espey who entered my office a few days later. "Do you know what you bought in *Fountains in the Sand?*" he asked.

"Indeed I do," I said. "A travel book nearly as good as *Old Calabria.*"

"No, no!" he exclaimed. "Did you notice how much of the manuscript was stricken through and rewritten? At least a third of the manuscript does not appear in the printed version."

"And so?"

"That suppressed third is the nucleus which Douglas expanded into *South Wind!*"

"Well," I said. "We bought a double 'sleeper'!"

Such was the discovery that Espey made, that probably due to the publisher's fear of libel suits, the satirical characters in Douglas's manuscript about Tunisia had been deleted, but not discarded by the careful Scot, whose habit was to use every last scrap of material in one book or another, and were expanded into what proved one of the most famous of modern novels. (Incidentally, the original manuscript of *South Wind* was among the treasures in the private collection of the late Doctor Rosenbach, and along with the manuscripts of Joyce's *Ulysses,* Wilde's *Salome,* and Conrad's *Lord Jim* is now part of the Rosenbach Foundation in Philadelphia.)

What of the third manuscript, that of *Old Calabria,* which the dealer had reported sold? I had to make a trip to New York before he would reveal the name of the collector who bought and still owns it. I have corresponded with her about UCLA's interest in succeeding her as the owner of this wonderful work. She lives on an island, and has confessed that marine borers have been at work; and in the interest of preserving Norman Douglas's manuscript from such ravagers, she may eventually accede to my wish that it join what has come to be the most complete of all Norman Douglas collections.

On the day when it arrives, after a deep bow to the donor, I shall go outdoors and plant a tree in the Scotsman's memory; possibly a eucalyptus, but if so and in deference to his distaste for the medicinal varieties, it will be one of the tall slim beauties known as eucalyptus *citriodora,* the sweet lemon-scented gum.*

* The tree will have to be planted at Bryn Mawr; the owner gave the manuscript of *Old Calabria* to the library of her alma mater.

STOP THIEF!

At one thirty o'clock in the morning of Saturday, March 5, 1949, I was enjoying the deep sleep of a librarian whose week's work is done—all cards checked, all orders placed, all books cataloged, all readers served, all returns shelved—when the phone rang. Blindly I reached out and picked up the little bedside radio and said hello. Then I knocked the lamp over. Our Siamese cats jumped up and began to purr for their milk. My wife slept on.

At last I found the phone and said hello into the earpiece. "Is that you, Larry?" a voice asked, then said, "This is the other Larry."

I recognized the voice as that of Laurance Sweeney, Superintendent of Buildings and Grounds at UCLA. "Good morning," I said.

First published in Wilson Library Bulletin, *December 1953.*

"Good morning to you," he replied. "We've had a little trouble—thought I ought to call you."

"Water pipe break in the stacks?" I asked.

"No, it's that book."

"THE book?" I asked.

"Someone tried to steal it." Sweeney chuckled. A long pause. "We caught him!"

"The devil take him," I said. "Where's the book?"

"Right here in my hand."

"Sweeney, you Irish angel! I'll be there in ten minutes."

I never dressed so fast in my life. By then my wife had an eye open. "Someone tried to steal the *Bay Psalm Book*," I said. "And Sweeney caught him."

"So what?" she asked, and turned over.

Driving through the empty streets to campus, I recalled the events which had led to a copy of the *Bay Psalm Book* being on exhibition at UCLA. It was the Rosenbach copy—the one that had toured the country on the Freedom Train—and the Rosenbachs, the Doctor and his elder brother Philip, had loaned it and the other Freedom Train documents to us for a Washington's Birthday exhibit.

Another copy of the *Bay Psalm Book* had made international headlines the year before when Doctor Rosenbach paid $151,000 for it at auction, for the benefit of Yale—the highest price ever paid for a book at auction.

The Rosenbach copy was said to be insured for $100,000, a story which the Los Angeles press had not overlooked. We had taken security measures. What had gone wrong?

The campus was deserted, the library dark—only the police office was lit up. Sweeney met me at the door.

"Where's the book?" I asked.

"Right here in my pocket," he said, bringing the calf octavo out and putting it in my hands.

"Good man," I said. "Very good man."

"Not me," Sweeney said. "Officer Frush. He's having a cup of coffee and will be back soon. Come see the crook."

He led me down the hall to a room where a student was sitting alone at a table, pale and haggard, his hands on the table. He was wearing handcuffs.

My first feeling toward him was of pity—his scheme, whatever it was, had failed, and he was due to sleep in jail. Not a good place for anyone to be. I suppressed this tender emotion and asked, "Are you a student library employee?"

"No, sir."

"What was the idea?"

Sweeney spoke up. "He says it was a fraternity prank—an initiation stunt—and that he was going to put the book down the return chute in the morning."

"What fraternity?" I asked the kid. "Not Phi Gamma Delta, I hope."

"A secret fraternity," he replied. "It was an initiation stunt."

"It didn't pay, did it?" I said.

"No, sir. I'm sorry I tried it."

"Come along," Sweeney said. "We're going to take you down for booking."

"Sweeney, you wit," I said. "You should be writing plays; that's worthy of Wilde."

The student got up and was driven away to the West Los Angeles police station.

Officer Frush returned then and I shook his hand in one of the warmest handshakes one man ever gave another. If Paul Frush was not an ex-cowpuncher, he looked like one—a tall, thin, sandy-haired, blue-eyed man, of few words and those in a Southwest accent.

We went to the library and he showed me what had happened. We had arranged the exhibit in one end of the reserve book room on the second floor, the windows of which had been sealed. The exhibit was shut off from the rest of the reserve room by a temporary plywood partition, which ran just short of the ceiling. We had the carpenters leave about a foot for cross ventilation when the front doors were opened. Crowds had attended the exhibition, including thousands of school children. Andrew Horn and Edwin Carpenter of our Department of Special Collections had compiled a hand list in record time, and Ward Ritchie had printed it even faster.

The books and manuscripts were housed in several dozen exhibit cases which the aforementioned staff members had scrounged from all over the city. The *Bay Psalm Book* was in a little mahogany case all by itself—a case without a lock, but closed by two invisible setscrews.

Invisible to all save this crafty student, who had studied the lay of the land. At closing time of ten P.M., he had concealed himself in the adjoining reserve area and lurked there for two hours while the janitors cleared the public rooms. At midnight they left. About an hour later, when he thought the building was cleared, the student somehow scaled the ten-foot plywood wall, squeezed through the crack at the top, and dropped down into the exhibit room.

STOP THIEF!

At one A.M. Officer Frush looked through the glass front doors and shone his flashlight about the room. He saw nothing amiss and left. Whereupon the student whipped out his trusty screwdriver, opened the case, took the *Bay Psalm Book,* and put in its place—of all things—a paper-bound Army language manual on Portuguese. With the loot in the pocket of his tweed jacket, the thief scaled the wall again, squeezed back through the crack, and dropped down into the reserve room. Here the windows were not sealed. He opened one. It squeaked slightly—and at precisely the moment when Officer Frush was leaving the building by the west side door, directly beneath the reserve room, on his way to circle the outside of the building. The student hoisted himself over the sill and dropped twelve feet into a bush of scarlet hibiscus. Soft and muddy earth broke his fall. He got up at once and made off.

Officer Frush approached at that moment and suggested he stop. The student began to run. Whereupon Frush drew his .45 and called "Stop! or I shoot!" Fortunately, for himself, the student heard the frontier quality in that voice—and also the click of the cocked gun. He stopped. Frush marched him to the station where he was searched and the book found. The captain was called. He then called the superintendent, who in turn called the librarian.

After hearing Frush's story and returning the book to the case, I went home and slept a few hours, then was back at the library, prepared to greet a thousand members of the California Library Association who were meeting on campus, with the Rosenbach exhibit as a special documentation for a program on intellectual freedom. I shuddered to think of the student having successfully made off with the book on the very morn of the meeting.

I did not believe his story of a secret fraternity prank. I was anxious also that there be no publicity.

The day went well and I thought everything was back under control—until toward the end of the afternoon. I was in the exhibition room with visitors, when one of the staff told me there was a man asking for me.

He identified himself as a reporter.

I drew him aside.

"What do you want?"

"The story," he replied.

"What story?"

"About the stolen book."

"What book?"

"O.K., Doc," he said. "I've read the blotter at the West Los Angeles station. I'm going to break the story. Wouldn't you like to have the facts straight?"

"Yes," I said. "Let's go to my office."

What happened to the student? What was his real motive? Through preliminary hearing and probation investigation, he stuck to his story of a secret fraternity stunt. I never believed it nor do I now. From what I learned of his background, I believe that he intended to shake down the insurance company for the few thousand dollars they would have paid for a no-questions-asked return of the book.

I didn't like the kid—who was actually not a kid at all, but a twenty-eight-year-old graduate student who had once changed his name—and liked him least of all the day he came to my office, when out on bail, and begged me to intercede on his behalf. I did eventually recommend probation—which he got—but that day I was ready to throw him out. He had come a little too close to making a monkey of me.

Two amusing footnotes . . . At the student's preliminary hearing in court, old Philip Rosenbach was put on the stand, white carnation boutonniere, perfumed handkerchief, patent-leather shoes, and all.

"About this so-called Boy's [sic] Psalm Book," the defense attorney began. "Is it not true that there are facsimile editions of it? What proof have we that this book in question is an original and not a facsimile?"

I thought Philip would have a stroke and die at eighty-three! He spluttered a full minute before he managed to say:

"I'll have you know, sir, the Rosenbachs don't deal in facsimiles!"

And the other footnote: the student was actually a transfer to California from the University of Oregon—and once, later, at dinner with a distinguished elderly friend of the University, I mentioned this fact, that the thief had been from out of state.

Quick was the comment: "See what happens when we let these foreigners into California?"

MY BIGGEST FLOP

COLLECTORS USUALLY WRITE of their triumphs, rarely of their defeats. This is the story of my biggest flop. It was a great idea. I never had a bigger one. It almost materialized. If so, it would have been my biggest coup. What was it? *A circulating copy of the Gutenberg Bible.*

Quite a few institutions own copies of the first printed book, but few allow people any more than to see it under glass. Exceptionally, Yale has loaned the Harkness copy at least twice—to the Golden Gate Exposition in 1939 and to the new Denver Public Library in 1956—and the General Theological Seminary flew its copy out to Dallas last year for exhibit in the new City Library. But usually when an institution owns a Gutenberg Bible, it stays putter than the building's cornerstone.

My idea was for the State of California to buy a Guten-

First published in Hoja Volante, *August 1957.*

berg Bible, to be circulated annually between the State Library in Sacramento and the University Libraries in Berkeley and Los Angeles. In changing locations, the Bible would have been consigned to the State Highway Patrol, with parade stops at public schools en route. The educational and inspirational benefits would have been enormous, particularly in the Far West.

I didn't get far enough with the idea to discuss it with the State Librarian or the University Librarian at Berkeley. If they had proved uninterested, I would have gone ahead and promoted it as solely a Southern California project, but the greater state-wide plan struck me as the only proper one for the greatest of books, and I feel certain that my northern colleagues would have embraced this bold scheme.

The idea was planted when I stopped in to see David Randall at Scribner's, just before we sailed for England in September 1950, and he reported having been the intermediary in the sale of the General Theological Seminary's copy of the Gutenberg Bible to a private collector in California. Upon reaching London, I offered this bibliographical tidbit to Messrs. Ernest and Kenneth Maggs, whereupon they gave me a later, larger, bit: the Seminary's faculty had prevented the sale, whereupon the California collector had acquired a Volume One only—the Dyson Perrins copy—through the good offices of Maggs Brothers.

Blocked in his sale, and not knowing of the collector's subsequent success, Randall had enlisted his overseas colleague's help to find another Gutenberg, whereupon John Carter had turned up the long-lost Schuckburgh copy, flown it posthaste to America, only to learn that the collector was no longer in the market for a Gutenberg.*

So there the matter stood, with an unsold Gutenberg Bible in a dealer's stock, probably for the first and last time in this century. Then it was that my idea germinated. When I saw the Bible at Scribner's on our way back to California in July 1951, I told Randall of my dream of making this Schuckburgh copy the California copy, to circulate between Sacramento, Berkeley, and Los Angeles.

Randall was first amused by what he thought was a pipe dream, and then when the smoke cleared a bit and the exciting educational opportunities of such a unique arrangement became clear to him, he shared my enthusiasm and the plan went forward.

When the Schuckburgh copy arrived at UCLA by Air Express, the amount of its insurance led the Railway Express Agency to deliver it by armored car. This nearly caused a riot on campus, when the students thought it a plot by USC to steal the Victory Bell. (I realize now that we could have done much to raise the educational tone in both schools to have substituted the Book for the Bell as the annual trophy to the winner of the Big Game between the cross-town rivals.)

I never told Randall of these shenanigans. He was already worried that the lad who tried to snatch the *Bay Psalm Book* and landed in jail would be out again and lurking in the hibiscus, ready to make off with the consigned goods. We of course gave it no publicity.

* John Carter, "Operation Schuckburgh," in his *Books and Book-Collectors,* 1957.

I shall never forget the thrill when we displayed the Gutenberg Bible on the table in my office for the benefit of the late Edward A. Dickson, Chairman of the University of California Board of Regents, to whom I first took my "circulating" idea. Former newspaper publisher, collector of incunabula, and lover of books and libraries, Mr. Dickson had immediately seen the possibilities of the plan; and I have before me as I write, the memo pages on which I jotted the promotional ideas which sparked from him almost faster than I could write them down.

It was agreed that the purchase price (somewhere between $150,000 and $200,000) be raised by a special appropriation bill in the State Legislature. Not only would it be a special bill, it would be drafted specially on vellum. There would be widespread newspaper publicity. The Bible would be shown to the people on television. There would be a sponsoring committee of citizens. Letters attesting to its value would be sought from national figures such as the head librarian of Yale, the Morgan, Huntington, and Congressional libraries. We counted on the bill gaining wide support. It would have taken a brave legislator to speak against the Bible, no matter how much it cost.

There was no quick way however to insure the sale. The California legislature would not meet until the spring of 1953, and this was the fall of 1952. Randall was under pressure, following the death of Charles Scribner, to clear the book out of stock, and he would not give us an option on it. We never did fix on the exact price. He wanted it higher. We wanted it lower. Naturally!

The Chicago Bible Society sought to buy it, and we

reluctantly had to pack it up and ship it off to Chicago. More armored cars. More gray hair for Powell.

The Windy City failed as the Golden State failed. Instead Arthur Houghton, Jr., bought the Schuckburgh copy, and followed the modern trend of trading in a used model, e.g., an imperfect copy of Volume Two only, which Randall later sold piecemeal.

So the dream is dormant, not dead, for as long as there remain copies of the Gutenberg Bible in private hands, institutions can hope, can hope . . .

ALL THAT IS POETIC
IN LIFE

"You say you want to give, not take; and if I feel the same, then what? Well, I do want to give too, but I also freely and gladly admit that I want to take what you have for me—all the strength and the sweetness, and the bruises too. If you don't know what I mean, read *Islandia*."

A cryptic reference. I was reading some unpublished manuscript letters of one of the best woman writers of our time, and these words of hers to a man gave me pause. They seemed to refer to a book, but by whom and when published I did not know.

The card catalog told me. *Islandia* was a novel by Austin Tappan Wright, published in 1942 by Farrar & Rinehart—a huge novel of one thousand and thirteen pages.

I began to read it that same night. It was a Utopian novel. My curiosity about it led me on a quest which now,

First *published in* Wilson Library Bulletin, *May 1957.*

four years later, still goes on. Here then is what I have learned about the book and its author.

The wartime was not an auspicious publishing time, but I cannot truthfully say that *Islandia* was overlooked by either critics or readers. It was given much attention by the leading book reviewers, all of which ran true to form: *The New Yorker* was faintly superior as only that island weekly can be. *Time* gave its usual treatment. *New Republic* looked down its socioeconomic nose. *Commonweal* deplored *Islandia's* anti-Christian philosophy.

The publishers pushed the book, and it had a moderate success. They even published a promotional booklet about the big book, written by Basil Davenport and called *An Introduction to Islandia,* which summarized the history of the imaginary country, reproduced maps, statistics, and vocabulary.

Then the book was forgotten in the war, went out of print, and became harder to find than Shakespeare's Folios, for the reason that whoever read *Islandia* would never part with his copy. In 1958 the publisher was led by public demand to bring *Islandia* back into print.

Why does it belong in the Utopian canon? Because it is one of the most completely documented imaginative works ever conceived, a book about a nonexistent country and its people, for which the author first wrote a 400-page manuscript history, a literature, a bibliography, a peerage, and a philosophy; created a landscape, geography, contoured maps, weather, statistics of exports and imports—nothing is lacking—and the result is a critique of our industrial civilization, Puritan morality, and business ethics, from all of which the author was a refugee, creating in *Islandia* a way of life dearer to his heart than that to which he was born.

Here are some other things I learned about *Islandia*. It was published posthumously, eleven years after the author's death, faithfully typed out on two thousand pages by his wife Margot, then sensitively cut to publishable length by his daughter Sylvia. It was commenced secretly by Austin Wright when he was a young Harvard lawyer, practicing in the Boston office of the great Louis Brandeis. Only his family knew that he was writing it. When Brandeis was named to the Supreme Court, Austin Wright took his wife and children and went West, clear to the Berkeley campus of the University of California, where from 1916 to 1924 he taught and practiced admiralty law. From 1924 until his death in 1931, at the age of forty-eight, Wright was professor of law at the University of Pennsylvania. He was a brilliant and beloved teacher.

None of his colleagues knew of *Islandia* until it was published, but their astonishment was not too great, for during his lifetime Wright was recognized as an extraordinary person, of deep sympathy, wide intellectual interest, and keen critical mind. The late Leonard Bacon, who was a member of the English department at Berkeley, writes in his foreword to *Islandia*, "He was a splendid example of the gay and engaging New Englander . . . he was on the threshold of becoming a great philosophical lawyer."

The *California Law Review*, in an obituary written by Orrin Kip McMurray, noted that his "charming and direct manner, his simplicity and devotion to duty, his enthusiasm for his work, and his willingness to serve, endeared him to his fellows. He had love for the School, for his students, for people, things, and causes. There seem to have been no rough angles in his character, no bitterness in him."

The obituary of him in the *University of Pennsylvania Law Review* penetrated almost to the heart of the matter: "Literature drew him strongly. His library was large and varied in its contents. One was given the impression that he was preparing to try his hand at some form of belles lettres if time and opportunity occurred."

How well he kept his secret!

Austin Wright had a rich intellectual heritage. His father was dean of the Harvard graduate school and a classical archaeologist, his mother a novelist. He was immersed in books and ideas from his earliest years. He had brilliant teachers at Harvard. He spent a year at Oxford, and pushed as far east as Greece, where he joined his father in the field. He was a kind of Renaissance man, akin to Leonardo in the diversity of his interests. He even learned enough engineering to lay out a railroad curve. His dearest pastimes were sailing and mountain climbing—two important things to note when we come to read the novel, for his Islandians are both saline and alpine.

Although Utopian—that is, about a way of life more ideally perfect than the one into which the author was born—Wright's Islandia was not a wholly imaginary world. In fact, its landscape is pure New England, of the White Mountains, and the Maine and Cape Cod marshes. Its architecture is Oxonian. Its women are physically the women Wright knew or dreamed of knowing. This is not science fiction, as written by H. G. Wells or Ray Bradbury, but rather the way a passionate Yankee, of keen and encyclopedic mind, humane sympathies, poetic sensibility, and ardent love-nature, found of eluding the strait jacket of Puritan respectability and domestic responsibility. It was commenced a couple of decades before *Lady Chatterley's Lover,* and Wright anticipated that other Puritan novelist, D. H. Lawrence, in the frank tenderness with which he wrote about sex.

And note this passage, in which the hero tells why he has chosen to return to Islandia, after a year's stay in the United States:

> Because the Islandian way is a better one. There a man is not split so that body and mind fall apart, the one going too far from earth, the other sinking too low in it. Here the labor which is regarded as the highest knows the realities on which men live only at second hand. We think too much about thoughts and not enough about feelings and things. Men specialize and deal with fragments and not with wholes. And our overintense brain life either desiccates the pure animal soul in man or makes an unmanlike beast of it. Desire becomes impure, perverse, a thing to be hidden and not to be faced.

That could be right out of a Lawrence novel. If Austin Wright had chosen a literary and not a legal career, we might have had a total work as varied as that of Lawrence. Instead, he put everything into this one huge volume, and because it is rooted in and true to life on earth, as we know it, and because the problems and desires of its characters are universally human, we read *Islandia* with absorbing interest. It is one of the great river-books of Anglo-American literature, a Mississippi of a novel which has the integration, coherence, and style which Thomas Wolfe lacked the art to give to his work. It is also a demonstration of the unpredictability of literature, which comes where and when it will, sometimes appearing like an artesian well in the dry academic landscape.

Austin Wright commenced to create his island world when he was a child, as revealed in a letter to me from his daughter Sylvia.

> Islandia started when my father was a small boy, when it was "my island." I have been told that he used occasionally to shut my uncle out of it [the reference is to Austin's brother John, who became one of the most distinguished geographers of our time], so my uncle then created his own country, which was called Cravay. Cravay, like Islandia, was thoroughly mapped, and I think had a peerage. When my grandfather, who was a classical scholar, died, they discovered an imaginary country among his papers. So to a certain extent it ran in the family. My grandmother, who was a novelist, also created a private realm for the purposes of her novels—a university town called Great Dulwich, though it wasn't a Utopia.

The opening pages of Islandia will convey a little of what this Utopian novel is about:

> In the year 1901, it was the custom at Harvard for seniors to entertain the incoming freshmen at "beer nights," where crackers and cheese and beer, to those who drank, and ginger ale, to those who did not drink, were served. To one of these I was invited with a random

selection of my new classmates. However much alike we would have seemed to older persons, we believed in our own heterogeneity, and having all of us social ambitions, feared meeting or being seen with the wrong man; but we also accepted the tradition that one of the greatest things in life was college and class spirit, and that knowing a great many men fostered it. We were therefore in conflict within ourselves, but did not know it, nor were our hosts aware of it either. Having no knowledge of anything naturally in common, we were all ill at ease.

A spectacled youthful boy talked with me in eager friendliness, but he revealed the fact that he was a graduate of a local high school. I made my escape and realized that it was far worse to seem to know no one than to be seen with the wrong one. I wished I had never come.

There was, however, another man in like plight. He was tall, over six feet, and heavily built. His face was too square, too ruddy, and too rugged for good looks, but it was strong and noticeable, with magnificently arched eyebrows; he had thick brown hair, that was black at night, parted in the middle, brown eyes with very clear whites, a strong chin slightly cleft, and a mature mouth. Because he looked like an athlete and therefore not socially compromising, and because his clothes were well cut, I dared and spoke to him.

His voice was deep and strong and, though anglicized, was peculiar in that every vowel and consonant was roundly articulated. I was embarrassed by its unusualness.

"How do you do?" I said. "Are you a freshman too?"

"Dorn," he answered. "My name is Dorn. Yes, I am a freshman."

"My name is Lang."

"Lang," he repeated and smiled, showing even white teeth. "That is like one of our names. Many of your names are hard for me to learn."

"Aren't you an American?" I asked, and hoping to please him, added, "You look like one."

"No, I am from Islandia."

His voice without being loud filled the room. There was a hush and many faces turned in our direction. None of us had ever seen one of his nation before. We knew that it lay, facing the Antarctic, on the edge of the Karain semicontinent in the Southern Hemisphere, that it was inhabited by an obscure Caucasian race with perhaps some dark intermixture, that it was pagan and hostile to foreigners, that the Islandians had rooted out the missionaries who had settled there in the forties, and that our school geographies gave it only a few lines because it was ruled by a peasant oligarchy, was agricultural and primitive, and had no trade.

Lang and Dorn become friends through their Harvard years, and Lang learns the Islandian language. Upon graduation he is appointed consul to Islandia, our government's object being to open this rich and unexploited country to trade. There is divided opinion about this in Islandia, however, with two of the ruling families on opposite sides. Lang gradually becomes converted to the side of the isolationists whose cause triumphs, falls in love successively with two Islandian women, becomes a national hero through his part in the defense of Islandia against the encroaching barbarians, and is the sole foreigner granted permission to stay in the country. He returns to New England for a year, however, and there becomes a successful businessman, before he rejects the American way of life, takes a New England girl, and returns to Islandia to the life of a farming family.

The book is long and leisurely, and dramatic in a restrained way. Once you fall under its spell, you are lost. I read it first in a headlong way, because I wanted to find out what happened, and wanted to learn what the woman had meant when she wrote, "If you don't know what I mean, read *Islandia*." This I did indeed find out, as I followed the novelist's delicate dissection of the love nature of three very different women, the Islandians Dorna and Nattana, and the American Gladys, for this man knew more about the subtleties of women's feelings than most men do, certainly more than Lawrence did.

Two years later I reread *Islandia* slowly, over a period of several months, absorbing a few pages at a time, letting its unusual qualities seep into and saturate my senses. It is a work of high intellectual power, of deep human insight, of penetrating social and philosophical criticism, and it is also a work of poetic and passionate tenderness. How does it differ from other Utopian books? Chiefly in the total way its author identified himself (and subsequently his readers) with the imagined country. Kenneth Oliver's remarks on this point are worth quoting. His essay on *Islandia,* in the *Pacific Spectator,* is the best thing written about the book. He wrote:

> ... No other author of a utopian novel has known the land of his creation as intimately as Austin Wright knew Islandia. Plato descended from the stratosphere of abstract philosophy to his Republic. He did not intimately asso-

ciate with its inhabitants under the conditions of life which he had created. Other utopian authors conceived fantasy-worlds where one or another great principle—economic, political, scientific, etc.—arose to dominance out of nothing, as it were, and waved a magic wand that suddenly gave perfection to eagerly awaiting man. Lewis Carroll, who *did* achieve intimacy with his dream world, did not give it the full depths of import which derive from the perfect interweaving of the real and the imaginary in a total panorama of life.

Wright found time, somehow, even from his professional life, to be himself in his imagination. More important—and more difficult—he found the means to interweave the work of reality and dream in such a way as to give greater magnitude to both.

The change from the American to the Islandian way of life is not wrought by magic, and its gradualness is why *Islandia* is a long novel. Nothing comes free to Lang; everything has to be earned. National prestige, family attitudes, business and professional ambition, sexual inhibitions—all the conventions of a Puritan upbringing, which Austin Wright himself never actually broke away from, because he really did not want to live outside of them, are eluded gradually by John Lang, as he becomes an Islandian in thought and deed.

Every great artist both eats his cake and has it too, and Wright was no exception. He married but once and had four children. He became the most respectable of all lawyers—an academic lawyer. He obeyed Flaubert's rule: live like a lamb so that you can write like a lion.

Islandia is a document of the artist's victory over himself and life. Writing it was Austin Wright's way of keeping his sanity in an obviously mad world of cutthroat competition, cancerous industrialization, sexual frustration, and worse; and the book is full of great health and joy for the reader who sickens of the movies, the comics, and Mickey Spillane.

Wright saw an Islandian way of life as the best of all therapies for the illnesses of our so-called civilization. What are some of these maladies? Ruthless competition, speed and hurry, noise, vicarious and superficial pleasures such as movies and TV, reliance on machines to do even our thinking, a primitive belief in the magic of naming things as a way of exorcising evil. Call it a virus, or an allergy; in either case, give it a shot, swallow a capsule. The worship of size alone (everything we have is the biggest, the highest, the longest, therefore the best), and a mania for reducing everything to statistics: traffic deaths or points after touchdown, pounds of turkey consumed in the forty-eight-hour period at Christmas, linear feet of barbed wire in Texas, and so forth *ad nauseam*.

Statistics are good only for what can be built on them, and Wright compiled the statistics of Islandia as a foundation for the temple of his book, as a prelude to the creative act. Our world makes a fetish of the fact as important in itself. Facts are unimportant in Islandia except as they contribute to personal happiness. Hedonism is the term which comes closest to describing Islandian philosophy—the doctrine that pleasure is the chief good and aim of action. But pleasure in the deepest sense of physical, mental, and spiritual fulfillment, not as harmful indulgence.

Our word *love*, which has to be coupled with adjectives to make its meaning clear, has no single equivalent in the Islandian tongue. *Amia* is liking or nonsexual love; *apia* is sexual desire; *ania* is the desire to marry; *alia* is love for family and place. The novel is a series of variations on these basic words, and what they represent.

The country of Islandia then is more of an emotional than any other kind of Utopia; and the novel *Islandia* is a love poem in prose, but of love as a state of wholeness, in which the entire personality is employed and fulfilled in the several relationships implied by the words *amia, ania, apia,* and *alia.*

To be whole, in a state of faithful believing—belief in oneself, in one's beloved, one's home and country—this was for Wright the *summum bonum*. He was a man with a profound feeling for life in all the factual, poetic, realistic, and imaginative wonder of it. The truth is in a letter to me from Wright's brother John K., the geographer, in answer to my question, Did his brother write his novel as the result of an intellectual thesis and after a specific regime of research?

> I doubt very much if he ever did any "research" for the deliberate purpose of gathering material for "Islandia." He wrote it out of his immense fund of memories and ideas derived from wide reading, and from a love of poetry and all that is poetic in life.

This poetic view of life permeates the book's thousand pages, leavening what in a prosy writer would be unbearable ponderousness. Wright sees life with Keatsian delight

ALL THAT IS POETIC IN LIFE

in its sensual qualities of color, texture, light, and shadow, so that the book is rich and real and rooted in physical life. There is much good talk in the book, as the American and Islandian ways of life are contrasted, there is a wonderful parliamentary debate, but there is also everyday living: horseback riding, swimming, and sailing, winter sports, wood-chopping, fence-building, carpentry and masonry, gardening and weaving. All of these activities Wright makes intensely real by the delight he takes in them, in the sights and shapes, the colors and configuration of the Islandian scene, there in that faraway country where the names of the people (Isla Dorn and Lord Mora, Hytha Nattana, Bodwin, and Stellina), the names of places (Loring, Miltain, and Bostia), and those of the seasons (Windorn, Grane, Sorn, and Leaves), form a vocabulary of lithe and liquid beauty.

We experience Islandia through all of our senses, not just as an intellectual concept, and that is why this Utopian novel is unusual, if not actually unique. What other author has told us so much about his imagined world, from the rigging on its sailboats to the color of its women's hair when they undress to go swimming?

To put it simply, this New Hampshire-born Harvard man, this erudite admiralty lawyer, this husband and father, this man Austin Wright was a poet; that is to say, one who sees wider, feels deeper, says clearer and simpler, that life is wonderful, is beautiful, is praiseworthy, no matter where on earth it is observed, whether in Islandia, New England, or in California. Austin Wright is a blend of Thoreau, Emerson, and Whitman, of Keats and D. H.

Lawrence, and he demonstrates the absolute unpredictability as to when and where genius will appear on earth. When wide knowledge is coupled with keen sensibility, and the person also has creative stamina, then we get a sustained work of art such as *Islandia*. Wright absorbed facts and feelings as a blotter drinks water; and he had the creative worm in his brain. He could not sleep until he had given his dreams form, if I may employ a paradox.

When Wright died, *Islandia* was a manuscript of several thousand pages. Did he regard it as finished? Yes. Did he intend to publish it? No, for he apparently believed in the Turkish proverb, that the highest good to which a man can attain is to be a genius and remain obscure. In a sense, his prepublication death was a blessing for him as a writer, for he was spared both New York and Hollywood, as well as the critics who rejected the very qualities which make the book unique and great.

Austin Wright died in a highway accident in New Mexico on September 18, 1931, while driving back to Philadelphia, after teaching in summer session at U.S.C. On that stretch of highway east of Santa Fe, beyond the Glorietta Pass and Pecos Pueblo, his Ford roadster skidded on the dangerous approach to the bridge across Bernal Arroyo, crashed through the railing, and fell forty feet upside down. His chest was crushed, and he died the following day in the hospital at Las Vegas.

It is a beautiful country roundabout there, in the Upper Sonoran zone of piñon and juniper and pink mesas, but his vision had transcended New Mexico. By the alchemy of art, this man had become Islandian, and I predict that he will be remembered longer as Farmer John Lang of the Lay River Farm in the province of Dole, than as Professor Austin T. Wright of Cambridge, Oxford, Berkeley, and Philadelphia, and for the reason that Life is short, and Art is long.

"The life of a good book," Gilbert Highet wrote about Juvenal, in words also applicable to *Islandia*, "is far longer than the life of a man. Its author dies, and his generation dies, and his successors are born and die; the world he knew disappears, and new orders which he could not foresee are established on its ruins; law, religion, science, commerce, society, all are transformed into shapes which would astound him; but his book continues to live. Long after he and his epoch are dead, the book speaks with his voice."

Read, and listen, and you will hear.

Part Two

EDUCATION FOR
ACADEMIC LIBRARIANSHIP

FOR A GOOD MANY YEARS the library schools have been the scapegoats of the profession. Williamson gave it to them good in 1923, followed by Reece, Munn, Mitchell and Metcalf, Butler, Carnovsky, and others, a series of indictments, confessions, reforms, and reorientations, blessed by the angel of the Carnegie Corporation. The results of this strange cycle were admirably summarized in 1946 by Wheeler and by Danton, in works titled with such words as "progress," "problems," "criticisms," "dilemmas," and "proposals." I have read much of the literature on education for librarianship, and found it for the most part to be a dull and introverted proceeding, lightened too infrequently by the humanistic flashes of the three M's: Munn, Mitchell, and Munthe. It is also a monotonous literature, unmarked by vigorous controversy. Even Chi-

Presented at the Conference on Education for Librarianship, University of Chicago, 1948.

cago, the pioneering school of the reformation, has not sustained its official literature on the level set by Pierce Butler in his eloquent tract, *An Introduction to Library Science,* a book which has unfortunately gone out of print.

The recent decades have seen the library schools adjusting themselves to their new affiliations with academic institutions, and under new leadership they now seem ready to achieve integration with these institutions.

I came to the writing of this paper with a certain objectivity. My only association with a library school had been as a student in one for a year. Since then I have tried to send my share of students along the road I took to gain the necessary certificate, and latterly as an administrator I have scuffled with my fellows for the cream of the yearly crop.

I have indulged in a minimum of library school baiting. Only once did I succumb to temptation, as in this paragraph written for the *California Library Bulletin*:

> In conversation with the head of one of our western schools I was dismayed by his glib classification of the current class by their grade point averages. I must confess ignorance as to which is better, a 1.6 or a 2.9 average. The latter is certainly the higher numerically. And we all know that six eggs make a better omelette than three. What we need is more librarians with good humor, good health, imagination, energy and adaptability. Do these qualities correlate with grade point averages?*

The bait was taken by one of the three Pacific Coast library school directors for whom it was laid. He wrote me in protest,

* "Academic Library Notes," V.9:4, June 1948.

The trouble with what you wrote is that some people are going to take you completely seriously, whereas the fact is that you would be about the first and loudest squawker if a library school sent you a graduate with a poor upper story! I doubt that "good humor" correlates positively with a high grade point average, but I'll bet that good health, imagination and energy do!

So I come as a librarian who, in his dozen years of professional life, has never taught a class or given a lecture in a library school, and who is employed in a university whose single library school is 400 miles distant. I am what is called a practitioner rather than a preacher, and yet I have come to regard myself as a participant in education for librarianship, by such activities as counseling and recruiting undergraduates, orienting and training and completing the education of new staff members.

I was impressed by this paragraph from Munn's report:

> That many promising young people coming from library schools full of initiative and enthusiasm are not given a chance to bring out their qualities of leadership is the fault of the libraries and not of the library schools. The first three months on the job are more important than the library school.*

I was so deeply impressed by this and by my own experience, that in my library we are conducting an orientation program for new staff members in order to get them safely across the danger zone between theory and practice.

I shall not attempt any definitive or inclusive statement

* Ralph Munn, *Conditions and Trends in Education for Librarianship.* New York, 1936.

on library school curricula, a technical area in which I am a novice. I shall instead offer some notes drawn from my own experience, re-examined in the light of what I have learned from the reading mentioned earlier and from my observations on visits to libraries in various parts of the country.

All of this by way of introduction. Let me now come to closer grips with my assignment by asking three questions and then attempting to answer them.

First, what kinds of librarians are needed by academic libraries? Second, are academic libraries getting the librarians they need? And third, what can be done by libraries and library schools to better provide for these needs?

Before answering the first question, what kind of librarians are needed by academic libraries, I must interpose another query: What are the functions of the college and the university library? One answer is that both are dedicated to the gathering of selective stocks of books and related materials; that the college library is primarily a teaching adjunct and the university library a research laboratory. To build collections and to use collections in teaching and research are the chief functions of academic libraries.

What sort of staff is needed to carry out these functions? First of all, some kind of administrative group is necessary. Should we look to library schools for administrators? Can library administration be taught? I would say that it can, in principle, not in practice. And who is to teach the principles of library administration? Head librarians on temporary leave or ones who have been permanently lured away from administration or personnel experts from other departments in the university—all three are possibilities. Columbia's new curriculum, as heralded in Danton's report and in writings by Carl White, should graduate librarians who will be apt candidates for administrative apprenticeships. I must say however that I am not favorably impressed by the inexperienced bright young librarian who is interested in "administration" to the exclusion of a preliminary mastery of the routine phases of library work. Good administrators are rare in any field of human activity, composed as they must be of aggressiveness and awareness in nicely matching amounts. The good executive sees minutiae with one eye, visions with the other. He is both galley slave and dreamer. Library schools should beware the current fetish of "administration" as it is worshiped in certain other so-called schools of public administration. Once more I find myself turning to Munn's report for a common sense paragraph, to clinch my point:

> It is nonsense to expect the one-year school to train leaders and statesmen; it has to train librarians to know and use books, bibliographies and catalogues. The school can at most attempt to secure students who have innate qualities of leadership, take care not to repress these qualities through excessive demands of routine work, give some vision of the purpose and the larger aspects of librarianship, and hope that in his early years of experience the graduate will have an opportunity to develop further his qualities of leadership.*

What about the need for the Ph.D. degree in academic

* *Ibid.*, pp. 22-23.

librarianship? In the field of university library administration, I would place administrative ability as the first need, and there is little or no correlation between it and scholarly ability. In the college library, where the administrative burdens are lighter and less complex, the Ph.D. is a more valuable asset, for it enables the librarian who holds it to teach on equal footing with the faculty.

If one of the library's chief functions is to build collections, then there is an urgent need for librarians who know books, how to evaluate them and how to acquire them quickly and economically. Books must then be prepared for use. Catalog departments need librarians who can read foreign languages, who can get to the heart of a book without reading it through, and who can recognize the necessity of applying modern production methods to the rapid handling of large quantities of more or less standardized materials.

Then we need reference and subject specialists to serve students and faculty in all the areas of the curriculum: divisional reference rooms, departmental and graduate school collections, and special collections of rare books, manuscripts, archives, maps, microfilms, tape and disk recordings, and so forth. Here, it seems to me, the important qualification is for subject knowledge and corresponding degrees, plus some education in library history, organization, and techniques.

The circulation and shelving of books is increasingly regarded as subprofessional work, which should be directed however by one or more professional librarians endowed with superior ability in managerial and public relations work.

To function properly, then, the academic library must be staffed by a corps of professional librarians with varying, not equal amounts of graduate education—managers, collectors, processors, interpreters, and curators.

Are academic libraries getting these kinds of librarians in the numbers required? They are not. There is a deficiency of superior candidates of every type. And yet a single year of two semesters in a library school is hardly enough time in which to attain high levels either of skill or knowledge. Nor does the new program in certain library schools, of granting an M.S. in L.S. after a single year of graduate work, strike me as likely to improve the situation. The University of California state-wide Library Council has gone on record as favoring an extra salary step for librarians entering the system who possess a master's degree in addition to the ordinary fifth-year library school degree. The extra step may also be recommended for staff members attaining advanced degrees through in-service courses of study. The Council does not recognize this new type of M.S. in L.S. as qualifying the holder for extra salary recognition.

What are some deficiencies in academic librarians?

The first is to me the greatest: too few librarians suffer from the disease Dibdin called bibliomania. We are paradoxically not a bookish profession. "Too busy to read" is our excuse, and it is a tragic one. To be sure, we do not need more dilettantes who "just love" books. Love is not enough. Give us librarians who have an overwhelming passion for books, who are bookmen by birth and by choice, by education, profession, and hobby. Properly channeled and directed, this passion for books is the greatest single basic asset a librarian can have.

Bibliomania is a passion capable also of refinement, offering the sufferer moments of exaltation and insight, such as this one described by an Englishman upon entering the library of the British Institute in Paris:

> Inside the big room filled from end to end, from floor to ceiling with books, I move slowly over the polished floor, unwilling to cast the pebble of my entry into the deep pool of silence among the bent heads. The calm brows see nothing, busy with making of one private world . . . And sitting there in the uninterrupted silence, I thought of all the people who had written those books piled so high in symmetrical layers cheek to cheek. They had poured out their hearts' blood, the anguish and the glory of something more than their minds, obeying blindly the call of the great inner voice that seems to sweep like a distant music through the air for those who can listen. An unending procession they were of skeletons now no more than an echo to be evoked through the strange deforming medium of the printed page. I saw their faces for a moment, wistful and uncertain if we, so far away in time and space, could understand . . . Human communication, of the living with the living, of the dead with the living, is one of the great mysteries of this existence. Mankind is a strange chain of minds encircling the earth with one common consciousness into which flow the thoughts and feelings of an immense number of other lives; he en-

EDUCATION FOR ACADEMIC LIBRARIANSHIP 123

joys the freedom of centuries though himself the slave of time.*

Coming down to earth again, let us consider some other deficiencies in the several kinds of academic librarians. Bibliographers or collection builders in order and acquisition departments too rarely are bookmen, with a feeling for the book as artifact and a knowledge of its content. They are not familiar enough with the international booktrade or with the history of book-buying and bookselling, or with the roles of bookseller, librarian, and faculty in the growth of library collections.

Catalogers fresh from library school (when they can be had) have not enough interest in anything but codes and subject headings. Knowledge of the history of cataloging and classification, of the modern viewpoint of cataloging as assembly line, and of the relation of the catalog department to the other library departments and to the students and faculty, are pitifully absent in neophyte catalogers. Too often they take an almost religious view of cataloging as an end in itself.

As for reference and subject specialists, I prefer them to come with one graduate year in library school, plus a master's degree gained from another year in specialization. To offset the present scarcity of such candidates, a library should allow in-service graduate study for its members whose work can be improved by intensive study, research, and thesis writing. Catalogers in all but the largest university library departments do not appear to improve their work and increase their output by further subject special-

* Wrey Gardiner, *A Season of Olives*, London, 1948.

ization; and in the large department the cataloger's assignment will dictate whether or not he should pursue in-service work, particularly in languages.

The ability of a librarian to achieve an advanced degree, or the mere interest in doing so, may indicate an effective concern with the essential work of the university or college and in the problems faced by the teaching and research faculty. A desperate deficiency is that of more librarians who have knowledge and interests and sympathy of the same kinds as the faculty. On every academic library staff I have an acquaintance with, I can count on few fingers the number of persons who can establish intellectual camaraderie with the faculty. Until this can be done by the majority of a staff, talk of equal rank with the faculty is a waste of breath.

Two more deficiencies in academic librarians are the inability to make concise written reports on library operations, and to report orally in departmental and staff meetings. The ability to communicate ideas by writing and speaking is an invaluable skill which is useful on all levels of librarianship, from junior member through department head to chief executive. Such skills in organization and presentation are partly native, partly acquired. Most library meetings are depressed by papers and reports poorly written and spoken, and of excessive length.

What can be done to overcome these various deficiencies in both quantity and quality? I am certain that the chief responsibility is that of the library and not of the library school. If the academic library is not getting enough properly qualified people to carry out its functions with complete effectiveness, it is in an admirable position to do something about it. Library schools derive most of their recruits directly from the campuses. The library is the heart of the campus, numbering among its clients, at one time or another, every superior student in attendance at the institution. What an opportunity to make converts in this proselyter's paradise!

The first step is to impress upon the staff the importance of recruiting and then of their individual and collective responsibility in interesting students in librarianship as a career. Here are excerpts from a memo on this subject which I addressed to my staff:

> Staff members should remember that our profession does not automatically perpetuate itself. A good measure of a library—and of each department in that library—is the number of students or clericals it has recruited for Librarianship. Each of you should ask yourself the question, What have I done and what am I doing toward peopling my profession? Here on this metropolitan campus, which draws young men and women from every state in the union, is abundant material. Every student who works for us is a potential librarian.
>
> The best recruits are those who are inspired by the librarians for whom they work to see in Librarianship a dynamic service profession. "Love of books" is not enough. Offer no refuge to the escapist; discourage the dilettante; pity the spiritual misfit, but close the door to the maladjusted. Librarianship holds no magic therapy. Its successful practice calls for normal (not average) men and women. Good health, good nature, good sense—look for these qualities.

We do not wish to recruit students all of one type. Keep the varied aspects of our work in mind when you are sizing up a prospect. Neither pure extrovert nor introvert makes the best librarian; most of us are hybrids, and properly so.

What else can be done to interest the student in librarianship? The first thing obviously is to operate an efficient library, to serve the student with promptness and good humor. It may be that librarians are most effective as recruiting agents when they are the least conscious of making an effort. Natural charm and friendliness, allied with efficiency, are great and rare virtues, but they can be encouraged and developed and made to flourish. This kind of courteous service should be extended initially to all library users, from the callow freshman to the sophisticated professor. It is a wonderful thing to experience and once seen is never forgotten.

Let me insert here a personal anecdote involving the head reference librarian in a university not far from Boston. I first visited the library when attending the ALA conference in 1941. I introduced myself as a junior member of the staff of a Western library. Six years later I returned, this time as a head librarian. The initial welcome extended me as an obscure staff member from a faraway place was indistinguishable from that I received when I returned on an official mission as the head of a library engaged in a joint project. I shall never forget this lesson in courteous hospitality regardless of rank.

The new student can be reached even before he enters the library by presenting him at registration time with a library handbook containing a welcoming foreword and hints on the use and enjoyment of the library. The student government can be encouraged to form a library committee, which will meet regularly with a library representative to discuss ways and means of improving library-student relationships.

A next step is to see that the student assistants employed in the library are, first of all, hand-picked from the large panel of applicants; then made welcome; given good training, fair wages, and promotional opportunities. I make it a point to get to know as many as possible of the students, at least by face and name, but this is not easy when more than a hundred are working at different hours of day and night. To each new student employee, at his home, I mail a letter of welcome—which says in part:

> It is important that you realize your responsibility in helping us give friendly and efficient service to all who use the Library.
>
> Remember that the entire Library may be judged by your performance. Be cheerful and pleasant to everyone. When off duty explain the Library's problems to students in your living groups.
>
> We want the Library to excel in service. I am counting on each one of you to see that we don't let anyone down. If you have to give a patron a negative answer, do it with a smile.
>
> Those of you who work in the Processing Departments are indispensable in helping speed books and pamphlets and magazines through for circulation and reference use. An unlisted item is of no use whatsoever to the public.

If you see ways in which our services and procedures can be improved, tell the librarians in your department.

I hope too that you will find more than a job in your work. Librarianship can be a stimulating and rewarding profession, offering a socially useful and varied career to young men and women. If you have not yet chosen your work, you may want to consider Librarianship. Any of the staff will be glad to counsel you at any time.

An effort can also be made to reach into the secondary schools and establish contact with the librarians there. We have addressed letters to them, asking that they call our attention to any of their graduates entering the university who may be interested in library work as a career and offering to counsel them at registration time.

Another effective recruiting device is an annual vocational conference on librarianship, to which are invited students and student and clerical employees, secondary school librarians and their student employees, and vocational counselors in the high schools and junior colleges.

The clerical or subprofessional group, which may form up to 50 per cent of the full-time staff, is another fertile field for recruiting, which should be recognized and systematically worked.

Wilhelm Munthe in his brilliant book, *American Librarianship from a European Angle,* urges that libraries be their own chief recruiting agencies and he advocates an apprentice system in order to insure grounding in library techniques before the student enters library school.

When I sought a formula for successful librarianship, I found most satisfying this one contained in Munn's report.

"It is," he says, "to a great extent dependent upon (a) general education with especial emphasis upon a wide knowledge of books, (b) common sense and other personal traits, (c) a relatively small amount of special library technique."* All I would add to this is a further year or two of graduate training in subject fields for academic and special library work.

There is general agreement that the best prelibrarianship education should be broad, liberal, and general. "But what constitutes such a general education?" asks a recent writer, and goes on to say, "Little, if any, attempt has been made to describe it in very concrete terms."**

We have attempted a concrete answer at UCLA in the undergraduate Curriculum in Prelibrarianship. The opportunity to introduce the new program came when a strong movement for a general curriculum reform was being successfully led by a progressive faculty group. With a bit of navigating through channels, we librarians succeeded in getting our own little boat under way and into clear water. A committee was appointed by the Dean of the College of Letters and Science to prepare a curriculum for undergraduates intending to pursue librarianship as a career. This membership included the Librarian, the chairman of the faculty library committee (a biochemist), and faculty representatives from languages and literature, social sciences, and applied arts. Next came a subcommittee of the Librarian and several of the library staff who had

* *Op. cit.*, p. 17.
** Harold Lancour, "New Training Pattern Looks Good," *Library Journal*, V.73:9, May 1, 1948.

shown an aggressive interest in recruiting; and a report was recommended, discussed, modified, and finally adopted. The Librarian is named as being in charge of preregistration advisers and he in turn has appointed his staff subcommittee as advisers. This curriculum is now entering its second year. The General Catalogue of the University describes it as follows:

> The Prelibrarianship Curriculum is designed to meet the needs of students who plan to pursue a general course in a graduate library school. The requirements of library schools and the demands of the profession indicate the desirability of a broad background in liberal arts subjects for students who plan to enter the general field of public and university library work.
>
> Students who intend to specialize in scientific, industrial, or other technical fields of librarianship should complete a major in the appropriate subject under the direction of the department concerned, rather than pursue the Prelibrarianship Curriculum. Students primarily interested in public school librarianship are advised to complete the requirements for a general teaching credential as described in the ANNOUNCEMENT OF THE SCHOOL OF EDUCATION.
>
> To be admitted to the Prelibrarianship Curriculum a student must file a "Prelibrarianship Plan" which has been approved by an authorized Library Adviser, and which meets the following general requirements:
> (1) One year in each of two of the following languages: French, German, Italian, Russian, Spanish.
> (2) Lower division courses:
>   (a) Requirements of the College of Letters & Science

EDUCATION FOR ACADEMIC LIBRARIANSHIP

   (b) Prerequisites for upper division courses selected by the student.
   (c) Recommended electives:

Astronomy 1	Geology 2
Bacteriology 6	Economics 40
Biology 1	English 1B, 31, 36A-36B
Botany 1A	Philosophy 2A-2B
Chemistry 2	Physics 10

   (d) Ability to type is recommended by many library schools and is generally recognized as an asset to the professional librarian.

(3) Upper division courses: At least 36 upper division units chosen from the fields listed below, with no less than 12 units in one field, and no less than 6 units in each of four other fields. The particular choice of courses should be determined by the student in consultation with a library adviser on the basis of the student's individual interest and needs. The recommended fields are as follows:

   I Art and Music
   II Education
   III English and American Literature
   IV Foreign Language and Literature
   V History, Economics and Political Science
   VI Psychology, Anthropology and Sociology

   Some 75 elective courses are listed in these six fields.

Here then are some concrete things an academic library can do toward bringing into the professional schools better qualified people.

What is the responsibility of the library schools in better training these recruits? Some of the curriculum reforms now taking place in library schools will have good results. I am not ready however to endorse those curricula which seek to commence professional training before the student has completed a course in general education. I believe that professional standards will be undermined and salaries lowered by the loosing of a horde of culturally immature technicians.

The schools need to improve their public relations. The faculty should come into closer contact with practicing librarians and bookmen. There is not enough intellectual traffic between library school faculty and librarians, except in those institutions where the school and the library administration are one—and then perhaps there is too much. The University of Illinois weekly colloquium is an admirable plan, by which the students and faculty become acquainted with and participate in discussions led by outstanding persons in the library profession and the book world. Students training for academic librarianship would benefit from a similar colloquium which would familiarize them with the workings of the university or college apart from the library.

The western United States with its widely separated oases of culture would benefit from institutes such as this, which blend theory and practice into closer harmony. May the wings of the foundation angel reach to the Rockies and beyond!

Another kind of isolationism has been increased by the shortage of librarians. This is the placement of most of a school's graduates in the region in which the school is located. My own staff is a case in point. Of a total of sixty professional members, forty-four are graduates of California and Southern California. Sixteen are graduates of thirteen other American library schools. I deplore this inbreeding in my own and in other libraries. In order to provide more varied and comparative experience for librarians, we need to consummate exchanges of personnel, with both foreign and domestic libraries. The invigorating life of a critically minded profession comes from members who have worked and studied and investigated in many libraries.

Lastly I will venture the opinion that a library school should be a place of intense intellectual radiation as well as a technical depot, a kind of station where in addition to an acquaintance with techniques the student is charged with high ideals, wide culture, deep humility, before he goes out to practice what has been taught. Teaching of this quality can only come from men and women who are seasoned and mellow, experienced and tolerant. When we look back on our library school year we are apt to recall it in memories of the teachers themselves, not of the courses they gave. Mitchell and Coulter symbolize California to those who were privileged to study with those two rare persons; and every other school in the land which lives in the memory of its students does so by its teachers—its Deweys, Windsors, Bishops, and Wilsons—not by its curriculum. What we must have if librarianship is to come of age is a great many more practicing librarians of strong character, wide culture, and active idealism.

MITCHELL OF CALIFORNIA

Whenever I am depressed about humanity, I console myself by thinking of the occasional brilliant success it achieves in producing from out of a million nonentities a personality of such individuality and influence as to make history and to achieve the immortality of remembrance. Such a man was Sydney Bancroft Mitchell, university librarian, library educator, horticulturist, writer, talker, legendary character even in his lifetime, which came to an end in his seventy-fourth year, September 1952.

Born in Montreal of Scotch-Canadian parents, educated at McGill University and the Albany Library School, Sydney Mitchell spent nearly half a century in California, a few years at Stanford and the balance on the University of California's mother campus at Berkeley. He taught a year in the Michigan Library School and traveled round-

First published in Wilson Library Bulletin, *May 1954.*

about the country and abroad, thus avoiding provincialism. He was a bilingual North American, liberal and tolerant, possessed of a tough mind and a tender heart.

The chronology and details of his life are to be found in his unfinished memoirs, and I shall not particularize on them here.* I prefer instead to seek the elements in his character and personality which made him such a rare and influential person. It is as a teacher of librarians, rather than as a librarian, that Mitchell is remembered. He could have been a chief librarian either in the university or public library field, but in the mid-1920's he left the associate librarianship of the University of California to found the University's first and only library school, and during the next two decades he built it into one of the country's few first-rate institutions.

I have not counted or classified its graduates. They include some of the country's leading librarians, and they are virtually unanimous in their devoted remembrance of Mitchell. Exceptional is the graduate who portrayed the Dean as a wicked character in her novel—and I have an idea that he might have been secretly as pleased with such literary recognition as he was with the honorary doctorate conferred upon him by Occidental College in 1946. Mitchell was showman enough to know that unfavorable recognition is better than none at all.

What makes a great teacher? Three necessary elements occur to me.

1. *Wide experience and knowledge.* A teacher, especially

---

* To be published by the Alumni Association of the School of Librarianship, University of California.

a teacher of librarianship, must be able to draw upon the total library experience of the race, and the more firsthand knowledge of libraries he has, the better is he able to relate and evaluate this experience.

2. *Deep insight into human nature.* He must know why people act as they do—from a desire for security, power, recognition, or a wish to help others, or a mixture of all.

3. *The desire to communicate.* A great teacher will not only be able to speak or write memorably, he will want more than anything else to communicate with others, to tell and to share.

I want now to examine these three elements of experience, insight, and communication, and see how they combined in Sydney Mitchell to make a great teacher.

The breadth of Mitchell's education, training, and experience kept him from being another frontier character. Although he became a Californian, with better perception and appreciation of the state than that of most native sons, Mitchell never lost a Scotch shrewdness and a Canadian plainness which saved him from the boosterism and exoticism that make so many Californians suspect by their more sober colleagues from east of the Sierra Nevada.

When he was at Stanford from 1908 to 1911 as Head of the Order Department, the Palo Alto university was really a country college where life was simple and unostentatious, and although the University of California at Berkeley, where he spent the next thirty-five years was already large and getting larger, the building of the university library and its staff was slow hard work. Everything that he achieved came from his own efforts. He never inherited a soft setup. He was truly a pioneer in Western library education, and he ended his career in a pinched wartime economy that reduced students and faculty.

By the time Mitchell came to teach young people the elements of librarianship, he had a practical background of three dissimilar university libraries—McGill, Stanford, and California—plus training and teaching in the dynamic centers of Albany and Ann Arbor. He knew books from reading them, libraries from working in them—and people? He knew people from affectionate firsthand knowledge. He was a student of human nature, a politician in the best sense of the word, a Yankee horse trader, a patient player of chess, with a loving touch in his moves.

Mitchell was not a scholar. He preferred teaching to research, and his instinct in this was right. Librarianship will not be advanced as a profession by the accumulation of a corpus of learned writing, as much as it will be the challenge and inspiration to would-be librarians of such leaders and spokesmen as Mitchell and his too few peers.

If he was not a scholar in librarianship—and this was by deliberate choice—Mitchell did prove himself a creative researcher in an entirely different line. He was one of the leading horticulturists of his time, entirely self-taught; and for the love of it alone he became internationally known as a breeder of iris and other flowers, he founded and edited for ten years the quarterly journal of the California Horticultural Society, and he wrote three popular books on gardening which had a wide sale and influence. He actually led two separate lives, as a librarian and as a gardener. A few of his friends were like him and could speak both languages. My wife is a true gardener, while I am merely a weeder and a waterer, a kind of garden drudge, and our conversation when we were with Mitchell was out of both sides of his mouth, as he modulated easily from shelf list to sow bugs. The Mitchell garden in the hills north of the Berkeley campus was one of the most beautiful in all the West, a fairyland in spring when the flowering fruit trees, the daffodils, and the irises caught one's breath with their loveliness.

Mitchell's insight into human nature was deep and luminous. He began by knowing himself and ended by knowing thousands of other human beings. His memoirs are peopled with characters. He had knowledge of some of the great ones of his time, including three extraordinary university presidents, David Starr Jordan of Stanford, and Benjamin Ide Wheeler and Robert Gordon Sproul of California. He knew Stephen Leacock at McGill, Melvil Dewey at Albany, and Thorstein Veblen at Stanford. Mitchell tells a good story about Leacock's way of working up his humorous material. A colleague was returning to campus after Christmas vacation and saw Leacock alone tramping through the snow on the deserted station platform, talking to himself, whereupon he crept up quietly behind Leacock in time to hear him say, "So the chemist said to his assistant, 'I can dispense without your services.' "

Another neat vignette in the memoirs is of Cook, the old porter of the Medical Building at McGill, who had probably a wider acquaintance with the medical students of his day than any teacher. Though his manner was austere he became a sort of foster father to them, and by the early nineties he had a unique place. It became traditional that there should be an annual parade and a ceremonial crowning of King Cook, with some chosen student delivering a laudatory address full of hits on the Medical School, the performance ending up with the presentation of tribute, a conclusion very pleasing to the tough and thrifty old Scot. But said tribute was always in unique form, one year fifty dollars in pennies scattered through a barrel of sawdust. Next year when the students realized how easily he recovered the money by dumping the whole contents into a tub of water, they substituted a barrel of molasses to hold the money.

I have said that Mitchell's insight into human nature commenced with a pretty thorough knowledge of himself. He was not a likely prospect for the success he eventually achieved. Most library schools today would probably reject a candidate such as Mitchell. He was badly crippled. Congenital dislocation of the hips made his legs too short and gave him a gait more rolling than that of most mariners. He was extremely homely, with thin blond hair, red face, and icy blue eyes.

Although he did not ignore his handicap and was always ready to refer objectively to it, his conduct was largely based on the assumption that being physically crippled was not as much of a burden as the mental handicaps of most people. After the first shock of meeting him, you found yourself as unconscious of Mitchell's crippling as he himself was of it. Certainly it never slowed him up. He played street games and football as a boy; he was a page in the McGill stacks; he drove a car and gardened.

And he married the one love of his life, Rose Michael of Montreal, who went with him by his side in all that he did, up to the day of his death. She also was a librarian and a gardener, she was a good cook, and best of all, she was a magnificent listener. Mitchell's emotional normality, which made him such a good counselor, was due to Rose. She truly made a man of him. They formed one of the best married teams this earth has ever seen.

In the notebook in which he outlined his memoirs, Mitchell listed his own personal characteristics, crediting himself, for example, with tenacity, patience, and tolerance, with self-confidence, a capacity for argument and long talking. He listed a dislike of self-pity and an incapacity for abstract thought. "Don't seek a fight," he noted, "and don't avoid one if it becomes necessary, divert an opponent rather than stop him, and never humiliate one you have beaten." On a campus noted for its politicians, Mitchell was one of the best. He was fast and rough and clean. He was honest and loyal. More than once the President of the University sought his advice, and on more than library matters.

Because of his wide experience and his deep knowledge of men and women, Mitchell became the most influential personal adviser Western librarianship has ever known. No other librarian held such a respected position. Former students came to him from far and near for advice both professional and personal. Nothing astonished or shocked him. Knowing the worst there is to know about people, he still liked them. He made few errors in judging people, and the one or two he did make were so colossal as to become classics. He knew more about libraries and librarians in the West than anyone else. Hardly a move was made, even in the smallest libraries, without Mitchell's hand somewhere apparent. People came to him and told him of their hopes and fears, their successes and failures, because they liked him and trusted him.

Typical was my own experience, in the last months of his life, when I was faced with a choice in my own career, a forking of the ways which meant a radical change if I took the divergent one. I could not seem to make the choice, so torn was I by the possibilities which beckoned in both directions. Then I did what many another had done before me: made my way to the hillside house of the Mitchells and put my problem in his hands. Expertly and lovingly he revolved it so that every facet was revealed; asking, telling, listening, talking, until finally it was crystal clear what I should do. He walked to the door with me and as we said good night, I saw his eyes cloudy with pain. He was old and ill and I had stayed too long. In another month he was dead.

It was the desire to communicate with others that completes the triumvirate of his qualities as a great teacher. He was egocentric and superbly self-confident, a natural showman and a born actor. He was a master in unwinding the tangled skein of human behavior. His stories went on for days, his parentheses within parentheses were fabulous. As he grew older and his graduates more numerous and more widely spread on the map and in various kinds of libraries, his epic narratives ranged higher, wider, and handsomer; and became connected and interconnected, with the old Dean at the center of the web, a most wide-eyed, farseeing, and benevolent old spinner.

His tales took off from the most unlikely points of departure, as for example once when we were eating in a San Francisco restaurant, a radio was broadcasting news which included a final item from a town in the Central Valley. Mitchell was talking steadily through the broadcast, but when the name of the town penetrated his consciousness, he shifted stories without a pause and took off on a lively account of library life in the Valley, from town to town, county to county, all the way from Red Bluff in the north to Bakersfield in the south.

I am one of the few students who never actually sat in a class of his. Mitchell was on sabbatical the year I was at Berkeley, and I came to know him only toward the end of the second semester, and then at his home. There and in restaurants and libraries and gardens roundabout the state our friendship ripened in the years that followed. I owe him more than I can say.

His classroom courses had names and numbers, but actually they were all classes in Sydney Mitchell. He was salty and humorous, the deadly enemy of the stuffed shirt and the phony. He hewed the truth as he saw it and the chips came down all over California. People are still picking them up.

The figure of Socrates comes to mind when I think of Sydney Mitchell. He was homely, even ugly, and he was wise; he dressed truth in anecdote; he was a tireless talker. Breakfast time beside a fire of bittersweet eucalyptus was a favorite time for talk—Mitchell talk, while his listeners swallowed vast amounts of tea. His favorite comment about me, and which he never tired of repeating, was, "That man's piped for tea!"

And even as Socrates, he walked with his students in the garden. Yes, he was a great gardener, this man Mitchell whose wife was truly a rose; he made flowers more beautiful, he made people more fruitful. His students are his immortality, and from them to their students will be handed on the truths he taught, and this is what makes a profession great and lasting. Mitchell of California! I pen his name with affection, and pride, and renewed faith in humanity of which he was such a magnificent example.

THE EXCITEMENT OF ADMINISTRATION

Up until now I have kept my mouth shut about administration, believing it is something one does rather than talks about doing. About books, however, I have done more than my share of talking and writing, so that I have come to be branded as a bookman. I am proud also of the administrative scars I bear, each one earned, I can assure you; honorable, not honorary.

There has been a good reason for all the talking I have done about books. No matter what one says about them, books can't talk back. Administration is different, is dangerous. Administration is people—living, breathing, talking people, one's very own people—and one cannot talk administration except in terms of people, who can and do talk back. I say "one" cannot. What I mean is, I cannot. The fact is there has been a great deal of non-

First published in College and Research Libraries, *July 1954.*

human, even inhuman talk about administration, about the skeleton of administration which is the organization chart, the span of control, the flow of work, and all the rest of the jargon of so-called scientific management and human engineering.

I must confess that I am uneducated in administration. The year I was in library school Sydney Mitchell was on sabbatical and no course in administration was offered. Besides, Mitchell's course, I was told, was not one in "Theory of Library Administration," but rather a riverlike monologue, flowing through areas of what he himself had done as an administrator and of what he had seen others do, always pragmatic, never theoretical. Fortunately for me, I did have his course later, unofficially, and without credit, taken at breakfast, lunch, and dinner, roundabout the West, in the course of a friendship that flourished until his death.

For seven years after leaving library school I was a simple bookman, uncorrupted by administrative responsibility; and then suddenly the good old days came to an end, and I found myself an administrator, in charge of a medium-sized university library poised on the crest of the postwar boom, equipped with nothing but instinct, confidence, and natural bossiness. If President Sproul had any misgivings about my overnight transformation, he was kind enough not to reveal them to me. My secretary *then* is my secretary *now*, and for two reasons: first, she had sense enough not to tell me what to do, and second, I had sense enough to learn a few things from her by keeping eyes and ears open, and mouth shut.

In the ten years since then I have seen my library grow to major size, in books, staff, and organizational complexity. We now have an administrative chart, a span of control, and a flow of work—all of this ex post facto—and we find ourselves willy-nilly an administrative training school.

It is not easy to keep from the schizophrenia which threatens the chief librarian. The bookstack is an alluring sanctuary from administrative trouble. And the temptation of turning into a practicing psychoanalyst, with overwrought faculty and overworked staff for patients, is easier to embrace than the comparatively austere life of a bibliographer.

In 1954 I was called to Columbia University for a semester to teach library administration. Every class must have a text. I looked around for one. When I asked one of my staff, whom I knew had taken a library school course in administration, for a likely text, he told me that they had been taught that the first modern treatise on the science of administration was by a Frenchman—Henri Fayol's *General and Industrial Management.* I straightway read it, and found it typically French in its inhuman lucidity, found it logical and true, as far as it went. Reading only this, however, would give one a wrong idea of the French, as I knew them from having lived as a student in a French pension and observed there the head of all French organization—the woman, the true head of the family. Monsieur Fayol writes like a bachelor who lost his mother when he was a baby.

No, this sort of dry-as-dust text would never do. I thought

THE EXCITEMENT OF ADMINISTRATION 147

of an earlier time, of my favorite century after the twentieth, the seventeenth. I knew I was running the risk of another scolding from my critics for playing the escapist, but I found myself ineluctably drawn to a seventeenth-century treatise on human engineering, a manual of conduct for public people written by a Spanish Jesuit. In understanding myself, my own religion of Quakerism has proved most helpful, but in understanding others, I have found that I could learn much from the Jesuits, the greatest of all administrative orders. This Jesuit treatise has been translated into a dozen languages since it first appeared in 1653. I first came across it twenty years ago in a bookish doctor's waiting room, and while being a bookman in Britain a few years ago, I found four earlier translations into our tongue.

It is called *A Truthtelling Manual and the Art of Worldly Wisdom,* and the author is Balthasar Gracian. It is composed of maxims—some would call them platitudes—which are worldly, practical, and timeless. Some of them are also rather cynical.

The quintessence of the advice which Gracian offers his readers might be summed up as follows: Know yourself, your weakness as well as your strength; know also how to conceal shortcomings and make a discreet display of your merits. Others, however, are at the same game, so *they* must be known as well. Penetrate behind their masks; be something of a clairvoyant, see through them and divine their thoughts. Do not exaggerate, and remember, also, that truth itself can sometimes be used in order to deceive.

Combine the subtlety of the serpent with the candor of the dove. Think with the few and speak with the many. Neither hate nor love on a permanent basis and remember that a friend turned enemy is the most dangerous of all foes.

I recommend this very human treatise to those who are practicing library administration. It is not recommended for beginners.

Here are the headings of some of Gracian's administrative maxims, with my own comments thereon:

Know how to discover each man's thumbscrew
   No comment.
Be a man who can wait
   Many things come to him who waits, but not always the ones he has been waiting for.
Know how to change your front
   Important when the potential donor to your library turns out actually to be a seller and not a giver.
Know how to make a good exit
   From the President's office when he says no, not a cent more this year. Get out even faster when he says yes.
Know how to say no
   To the Business Manager when he suggests you give over half of the catalog department's space to house an irrelevant activity.
Know the meaning of evasion
   No comment.
Allow yourself some defects
   Minor ones, of course.

THE EXCITEMENT OF ADMINISTRATION 149

Know how to further another's plan to accomplish your own
  Regional co-operation.
Without lying, do not speak the whole truth
  Might have something to do with annual reports and budget requests.
Discover someone to help you shoulder your misfortunes
  Associate Librarian.
Know how to let blame slip upon another
  Assistant Librarian.

What happened to this oracle named Balthasar Gracian? With his treatise in his hand, he must surely have ended as Governor of Granada or Captain of Castile! Not quite. The fact that he was a bookman got him into trouble. He published works critical of his superiors, and when they ordered him to cease and desist, he stubbornly kept on doing it, in fatal contrariness to his own advice to others. How very human! He was stripped of his offices and sent into exile, and even there his desk drawer was searched for evidence of disobedience.

I do not want to end on a note of cynicism or futility. I like administration. Running a library (and that means knowing also when to run from it) is my idea of heaven-on-earth. What are the qualities I am going to tell my students are needed for success as a library administrator? Here is a brief list, each with its converse:

Know how to speak—and how to listen.
Know how to write—and how to read.
Know how to work fast—and how to do nothing.

Know how to delegate—and how to retain.
Know how to credit others—and how to take blame.
Know how to change your lens from wide to narrow—and how to be blind.
Know how to win loyalty—and how to be loyal.

If anyone knows of such a paragon, have him write to UCLA. We have an opening at the bottom, with nowhere to go but up.

LEARNING TO TEACH, TEACHING TO LEARN

WHAT WAS IT LIKE to be at Columbia University during her bicentennial celebration? It was the most exciting thing that has happened to me since February 1, 1938, when I went to work at UCLA. To rub shoulders on campus, and eat together in the faculty club, with such men as Henry Steele Commager, Allan Nevins, Gilbert Highet, Robert "Middletown" Lynd, and President Russell of Teachers College and President Kirk of the entire University, was a rewarding experience.

The bicentennial theme—made familiar by the special blue-and-white three-cent stamp and by many programs and publications—was Man's Right to Knowledge and the Free Use Thereof—and the stand on freedom by Columbia University and its former president was a constant inspira-

First published in California Librarian, *October 1954.*

tion, particularly in 1954 when political gangsterism hit a new low.

To be on Morningside Heights meant that the chimneys of Harlem smoked in the east, and the tower of the Riverside Church ruled the west, that thousands of students poured in and out of the subway, that the sky was full of planes westward bound from La Guardia Field, and that I was the fortunate occupant of an office on a high floor of the Butler Library, where the Columbia School of Library Service occupies spacious and practical quarters. Mother of all American library schools, founded by Melvil Dewey in 1887, the Columbia school has a proud tradition, and is reinforced by a vast collection of library literature.

I had never fully realized the extent of library literature —books, pamphlets, periodicals, bulletins, leaflets, ephemera of all kinds, in many languages—organized and arranged, bound and cataloged, with adjoining stacks, alcoves, reading rooms, and reference desk, under the general supervision of our former colleague at the Huntington Library, Roland Baughman, and the immediate direction of Darthula Wilcox, a former Texan, who is one of the best librarians I have ever met. What do I mean by "best"? Miss Wilcox not only knew what she had and where it was, she was also full of active good will toward those who needed help.

The Columbia faculty was well rounded in theory and practice, and included kindly Dean Carl White, bibliographical Allen Hazen, dynamic Maurice Tauber, inquiring Robert D. Leigh, bookish Ray Trautman and Bertha Frick, medical Thomas Fleming, and architectural James

Van Derpool, the versatile Misses Alice Bryan, Winifred Linderman, and Hilda Grieder, and the late Miriam Tompkins, whose sudden death early in the semester grieved her many students past and present. A memorial service held in the Episcopal chapel on campus, an afternoon of bitter wind and cold, was deeply moving.

As the time of my appointment drew near, I became increasingly nervous, for I had been critical of library education, ever since I received two semesters of it in 1936-37; and now it meant either "put up or shut up." I have never been without initial nervousness before facing an audience (which fortunately dissolves in the flow of words), and the week before my first class was spent in wondering why this boy from Westwood ever left the barley fields of home. The interestedness, and the bookishness, of my class and their responsiveness to the challenges I threw down ("We're here to work and to learn and to believe.") soon reassured me that I had made no mistake in responding to Columbia's call.

The area of my teaching—library administration—would not have been my first choice if I had been able to choose my courses; and yet on second thought I was glad to have an opportunity to preach about what I had been practicing for ten years. It is good to be known as a bookman, and yet my interest in administration is active and vital, and I am proud of the organizational accomplishments of my decade as head of the UCLA library system.

The basis for my course was the syllabus prepared in 1950 by Lowell Martin, called "Theory of Library Administration," to which I made modifications, and additions, such as sections on library leaders and library literature. Thirty-seven students signed up for this optional second-semester course, and only two dropped out after the first day, both foreign students who probably had difficulty with my California accent. Other foreign students remained, however, along with men and women from all parts of the United States, with an average age somewhere in the twenties and about equally divided between academic and public library interests. My procedure each Monday and Wednesday, from 10:00 to 10:50 A.M., was to open the class with a short reading from a book or a periodical (often from Emerson, a great theoretical administrator) aimed to reiterate my belief that books are basic and that it is wicked to call a library a "materials center."

I would lecture on the day's assignment, employ spot case reports and occasional quizzes, and then serve as referee in free-for-all discussion. The excitement of librarianship filled the room, as lively give-and-take ensued among the students themselves and between them and me. Not all of them were taking the course because they intended to be administrators; a number merely wanted to find out what it was all about. So did I! *Being* an administrator is someways easier than *teaching* how to be one. I believe that I benefited from the discipline of being compelled to concentrate my knowledge into the framework of the week's comparatively few hours of classes, and to focus my heterogeneous experience so that it would burn with maximum intensity during the span of fifty minutes.

I also conducted a seminar of eight doctoral candidates in Some Administrative Problems in Large Libraries, and this weekly two-hour session was always over too soon. Topics dealt with included Acquisitions Policies in Engineering Libraries; Classification Schemes as Influenced by the Size of Collections; the Documents Expediting Project; the Organization of the New York, Queensborough, and Brooklyn Public Libraries; Co-operation Among the Queens, Brooklyn, Hunter, and City College Libraries.

Administration is not something that I taught as an abstract set of rules, or as a purely theoretical matter, but I sought rather to ground my students in what it means to be a librarian: that librarianship is a humane art, not a mechanistic science, that we were in a school of library service, not science. I insisted that librarianship is a calling, similar to the ministry, that gives rich returns to those who give their lives to it, and that the spiritual rewards of librarianship should not be minimized in this time of emphasis on rising salaries, new buildings, and all the physical aspects of our work. I preached the only gospel I know: that books are basic and that people are good, and that to work with them both is the best of all lives. And furthermore that a person truly becomes a librarian, not when he is a certificated graduate of a library school, or has finished x-number of years of work, but rather at that time when he speaks with inner or outer voice and says, "This work with books and people is the best of all work —I do it because I love it—and want to go on doing it until I die."

I cannot conceive of any course in librarianship which ignores books, and I found the bookish approach to administration both practical and popular. Libraries are administered to provide a gracious and economical union of people and books. This doctrine brought us all close together, so that when the semester ended I was warmed by the *esprit de corps* that fired the group, and will always remember the parting remarks of one of the students who said, "You have made us come to be fond of each other by the give-and-take in class."

Instead of a final examination each student wrote the annual report of a library he had chosen or created at the beginning of the semester, and to which from week to week the various aspects of administration were applied. These ranged from a business research library in Chicago to a university library in Egypt, common to all of which were the essential elements of good administration: efficiency, economy, imagination, humaneness.

What did I learn from my semester at Columbia? One of the chief things is that the West needs a library school of the stature of Columbia, with a strong supporting library of its own, the best and most versatile faculty that money can secure, with day and night and year-round facilities, so that people at work can take more training without giving up their jobs.

I have been thinking about a library school which, in addition to a strong central base, would offer extension work in librarianship out in the wide and beautiful field of the Southwest. Recruiting is one of our greatest problems, and a branch library school on wheels—a combination bookmobile, mobile classroom, and sound truck—might prove to be a good recruiting as well as teaching device. The concentration of the state's population (and source of tax revenue) in Southern California has led to the duplication at UCLA of the professional schools which were once found only at Berkeley. Librarianship will inevitably follow.

What I learned at Columbia was both exalting and humbling, and I pledge my best efforts to the improvement of library education in California, whether it be public, private, or parochial, or a combination of all three. We have great traditions to build on and leaders to follow: I think of Sydney Mitchell and Helen Haines. I am glad to observe that both the California Library Association and the School Library Association of California have created committees on library education.

I have had the good fortune in the past year and a half of meeting librarians at home in twenty-one of our forty-eight states, and I say again, librarianship is a kind of universal brotherhood, and the language we speak is infinitely translatable. I am glad and proud to be a librarian, and I believe that joy and pride in librarianship are two of the chief things to be transmitted to our students and successors.

LIBRARIANSHIP IS A CALLING

In setting forth the responsibilities of Southern California in Southwestern library development, in participation with librarians from Arizona and New Mexico, I want to begin by recalling words spoken at Chicago in 1954 by Patricia Paylore of Tucson when she described us as "ancient enemies"—Arizonan, Angeleno; she the erstwhile bookless girl from Clarkdale, I the custodian of the Clark Library, that fair monument built with the sweat and tears and copper of the United Verde company town.

When he heard that I had invited neighboring librarians to Los Angeles for a regional conference, another Southwestern librarian, formerly in New Mexico and now in Oklahoma, sent these words of warning:

> Actually New Mexico and Arizona cannot enrich the already enormous library resources of Los Angeles, and

Read at Rockefeller Conference on Libraries in the Southwest, Occidental College, 1955.

you are more likely to find the region a territory for service and perhaps leadership, if you can be humble enough. Those are very proud and independent people out there, even though they have little. They probably would welcome you and be appreciative of your interest, but I have the nasty suspicion that the rest of Southern California will not share your enthusiasm and interest, and I doubt whether you can get far if Los Angeles as a whole is indifferent. Indifference would offend Arizona and New Mexico, and prevent any real getting together.

There was no use in my pretending to be a humble person. Nor was I the one to repent for the biblio-predatory sins of Henry Huntington, Will Clark, and Charlie Lummis. Their research materials are in Southern California, and properly so. A good library gains strength from proximity to other good libraries. The complex of libraries in Southern California—this common pool of books—illustrates our national motto: *e pluribus unum*. These great rare-book libraries would be all but deserted and probably neglected, if they were situated in the parts of the Southwest from whence came the natural resources that made them possible. They are not the kind of libraries needed by the arid regions.

But that is not the complaint of our neighbors across the river. What they resent is the fact that so much was taken from their soil by their sweat to enrich Southern California, and so little left in return: a statue of Senator Clark in Butte, an abandoned smelter in Clarkdale. And on top of all this, we soak up more and more of their water in our urban blotters.

It was one of the first Southwesterners, Mary Austin, who prophesied ruin for Los Angeles because of the way in which the Angel City played the devil with the Owens Valley. And now the enemies of our progress are found at all points on the river, from sandy Yuma to the crystalline headwaters, all passionately convinced that we are greedy and rapacious, and hoping that we may yet smother in our own smog.

I do not apologize for this display of "manifest destiny" which Southern California is putting on, and which has made us the most hated of all big cities. It seems to me inevitable, human, historical. But we should not forget the fate of other hated cities of history: of Nineveh and Tyre, of Carthage, and Rome, and Berlin; nor should we ignore the verses of another California prophet, Robinson Jeffers, such as his poem called "Summer Holiday":

When the sun shouts and people abound
One thinks there were the ages of stone and the age of bronze
And the iron age; iron the unstable metal;
Steel made of iron, unstable as his mother; the towered-up cities
Will be stains of rust on mounds of plaster.
Roots will not pierce the heaps for a time, kind rains will
    cure them,
Then nothing will remain of the iron age
And all these people but a thigh-bone or so, a poem
Stuck in the world's thought, splinters of glass
in the rubbish dumps, a concrete dam far off in the mountain ...

Thus when I say that Southern California has regional responsibilities because of the material enrichment it has received from the region, it might be thought that I am moved by fear rather than by humility. No, I don't think any overwhelming fate is imminent, although I must confess to sleeping better since we moved from the neighborhood of the Douglas plant to the coast beyond Malibu. I have read Ray Bradbury's *Fahrenheit 451*, and I have also read Ward Moore's *Greener Than You Think,* in which Southern California is overrun by devil grass; and frightened as I am by these books, and by Huxley's *Ape and Essence,* I find myself, in spite of their warnings, planning for at least a generation ahead. It is more than blind optimism which moves us to confer with our neighbors. There is belief and faith, and perhaps a grain of humility.

I do not propose to dwell on the obvious ways in which the libraries of Southern California can share their wealth with the Southwest. This is being done daily by interlibrary lending, by bibliographical services of various kinds; and the state-wide University of California is properly one of the leaders in this.

My text is based rather on two words in that Southwesterner's letter to me on the need for humility: they are *service* and *leadership*. What can we in Southern California's libraries do to serve and to lead the libraries of the greater Southwest to a richer life of wider usefulness? I turn again to Patricia Paylore for my answer, and propose that we accept the challenge in these words of hers:

"I mean simply that in the arid Southwest, it takes more to be a good librarian than elsewhere. An ordinary man just won't do. For it takes fortitude and a crazy kind of stubbornness to go on believing in books and libraries and their power to transform and illuminate, when you have to battle against odds . . . I dare say you in California had someone somewhere in the beginning who had what it took—maybe Jim Gillis or Charlie Lummis. But these heroic characters are accidental.

"My query is," she continues, "what kind of people are being trained now for what kind of librarianship that there are so few who measure up. Are there no more pioneers? Is the frontier really gone? I say no! And I challenge the library profession to breach it."

There is the challenge that I propose we Southern Californians accept. And how? By the establishment of a wholly new kind of regional library education program that will recognize the dual nature of library education: that what we teach is matched in importance by whom we teach it to. In other words, recruitment is just as basic as training.

For nearly ten years we have had a prelibrarianship curriculum at UCLA. I helped start it, and I have had some good things to say about it.

A shortcoming was that librarians were advising students, but no librarians were teaching, and thus having direct contact with undergraduates. The picture changed in 1953. The English department offered for the first time a course in children's literature, required of all majors, and it was taught by a librarian—by our Elementary School Librarian Winifred Walker; and she was succeeded by Frances Clarke Sayers. Students flocked to these two librarian-teachers, and some of them have been drawn into school and children's library work.

It seems clear to me that we need teacher-librarians or

librarian-teachers in all our undergraduate schools, infecting students with the bookish virus, infusing young men and women of unusual talents with enthusiasm, and the belief that librarianship offers rich opportunities for personal satisfactions and wide opportunities for public service. If we believe that librarianship is a calling, then should we see that the call is heard, clear and ringing, in all the centers of student population throughout the Southwest.

What we propose then is a regional program of library education which will draw into the teaching of undergraduate courses on books and society more such forceful personalities as Dorothy Drake of Scripps, Frank Baxter and Althea Warren of USC, Frances Clarke Sayers of UCLA, Erna Fergusson of New Mexico, and Patricia Paylore of Arizona. A flexible curriculum could be developed by a special committee of the state library associations of Arizona, New Mexico, and California; a pilot course might be the one on "Libraries and Learning" which we inaugurated in the upper division at UCLA.

Recruits from the colleges and universities of the Southwest could be sent to graduate library schools throughout the country, but I truly believe that the Southwest sorely needs one publicly supported graduate library school, and furthermore that the University of California at Los Angeles is the only state-funded institution in the region which can afford to found and to operate a major graduate school, with a minimum enrollment of one hundred students.

I believe also that the population growth of the Southwest has disproved Robert D. Leigh's conclusion that California cannot support three major schools. A later survey made at UCLA indicates that Southern California is not producing enough librarian recruits in proportion to its total population.

Greater San Francisco, the so-called Bay Region, now numbers 2,500,400 people, from which the Berkeley library school enrolls one in every 60,985. Greater Los Angeles, called so many things, now has 5,221,200 inhabitants; and yet from this massive population the USC library school draws only an estimated one from every 124,314 people.* Thus from a population twice as large as the north, the southern school is recruiting only half as many librarians.

Another fact shown by our post-Leigh survey is that in the national picture Los Angeles has one of the lowest ratios of local students enrolled by its local library school.

I see two reasons for the low ratio of librarians being recruited from our large population: the first is that the one low-cost major library school is four hundred miles away. The other may well be the cost of tuition at USC.

Founding a school at UCLA should not materially affect Berkeley. It does not depend on Southern California. In 1955 only three UCLA graduates were in the total of seventy-four students at University of California, whereas the library school in the north recruited thirty-two students with the University of California bachelor's degree. One after another the professions have recognized

---

* Estimates of the Division of Budgets and Accounts, Department of Finance, July 1, 1955.

the geographical facts of life in California, and pressed successfully for the establishment of publicly supported facilities in both of the two great and widely separated areas of population. Librarianship is among the last, and the need is greater every year, as California overtakes New York as the most populous state, and the Leigh report is left behind.

What effect would a school at UCLA have on that at USC? Some may smile when I sincerely declare that it would increase their enrollment. The evidence of the recently founded UCLA graduate schools in law and social welfare does not show a significant reduction in the enrollment of those graduate schools at USC. National trends rather than local conditions determine the size of professional schools—and the national trend in librarianship is one of increasing shortage of trained librarians.

From where then would UCLA draw its library school enrollees? A graduate library school there will draw its enrollees primarily from that student body; and from students not going into librarianship; and from the other colleges and universities of the Southwest whose students wish to go to an inexpensive major school close to home; and from all over the world. Just as the Westwood campus is now a mecca for foreign students, so would a local library school draw students from Latin America, Europe, and the Orient; and its curriculum should be strong in courses on international as well as regional librarianship.

Let me recall Edwin Castagna's words:

> We need to consider the problem of training librarians specifically for service in the Southwest. A library school

able to recruit intelligent and public-spirited young people from Southwestern states, able to train and motivate them to go back and serve their own areas would be performing a fine service to the profession. Such a school might very well take its students on extended field trips and let them work in various sections of the Southwest, so that they become really familiar with the broad problems and possibilities of the whole area.

During recent years I have journeyed into Arizona, New Mexico, and Texas, and have spoken to librarians and readers in Tucson and Phoenix, in El Paso, Albuquerque, Santa Fe, and Los Alamos; and I have learned that we in Southern California, from San Diego to San Luis, and from Inyo to Hueneme, may have cornered the region's books. but not its wisdom. There is more of the essence of the Southwest in the single thin volume by Haniel Long called *Interlinear to Cabeza de Vaca* than in a stack-level of learned sets; and in his novel called *Grant of Kingdom,* Harvey Fergusson has done what few historians succeed in doing: made the past to live and to breathe, its people to love and to die.

And as a result of what has been learned on these Southwest *entradas,* I believe that part of the required work in the new library school should be a field trip over Southwestern itineraries—required of students and faculty—with stops at campuses and schools, as well as at libraries; and after having read those determining books: *Sky Determines, The Delight Makers, Blood Brother, The Rainbow Trail,* and *The Wonderful Country.*

Too much of the recent literature of library education

LIBRARIANSHIP IS A CALLING

is concerned with the degree structure, with curriculum patterns, with admission procedures. I do not intend to add to it. 'Tis the gift to be simple that I seek, and I believe that we have lost sight of the moral issues, of basic principles, of spiritual values. Since the death of Sydney Mitchell and the retirement of Helen Haines, library education in California has not had spokesmen to match them, although in Southern California we have had a succession of gracious and sincere library educators in Mary Duncan Carter, Lewis Stieg, Frances Spain, Harriet Howe, and Martha Boaz, with all of whom we have worked in harmony.

Gillis and Lummis were great pioneers. But they were not accidental figures. The times produced them, just as the next generation produced an Asplund, a Mitchell, and a Haines. In our present need I have no doubt that there will be leaders to rise up and lead us; and the lesson of American life teaches us that our leaders are as apt to come from country as from town, from Snowflake or Sedona, from Cloudcroft or Chama. Our vision should be even wider than the limits of Los Angeles. We have more to learn than we have to teach.

These things need to be said over and over: librarianship should be a hard discipline, demanding concentrated study and work in the field; and it should be a continuing discipline, a matter of lifelong learning. Librarianship should be as consuming a calling as the ministry and medicine, to which its servants dedicate and give their lives, and in the giving find themselves, renewed and reborn even as they are consumed—a consummation devoutly to be taught.

"A man is at his best," said Will Levington Comfort, "in those periods in which self-interest is lost to him. The work in which a man can lose the sense of self for the most hours each day—that is his especial task. When the workman gives forth the best that is in him, not feeling his body, above all its passions and petty devices for ruling him, concentrated upon the task, a pure instrument of his task and open to all inspiration regarding it—that man is safe and superb.

"Each workman finds in his own way the secret of the force he represents. He is an illuminated soul in this discovery. It comes only to a man when he is giving forth, when he is in love, having lost the love of self. Giving forth purely the best of self, as the great workmen do, a man is on the highway to the divine vocation which is the love and service of humanity."

It is our destiny in Southern California to accumulate a great wealth of people and the accompanying material resources of occupations and pleasures and education. *Richesse oblige.* Our responsibilities are many and we must fulfill them, lest we be punished by Mary Austin's angry God. In librarianship these responsibilities transcend the mountains and the desert and the river, and go out to all the people of the Southwest who cannot live alone on sun and water, people who require books to feed their intellectual needs and their spiritual hungers. Librarians can be a kind of priesthood to minister to bookless people; and part of our responsibility here where we have great educational resources is to train a new band of missionaries, of coarse-robed and sandal-shod librarians who will gladly go on unpaved roads, and whose workday will be from sun to sun, and who can extract nourishment from a few figs and pamphlets. There are riches to be found beneath the minimum wage; there are refreshments not served at the coffee break; there are rewards unseen by Recordak. We who have found them in library work must tell young people about them, must transmit to our successors our faith in books as good medicine for the maladies of modern life, as good tools in education, as joyful companions, and as the best of solacers in times of sorrow.

This may not be a doctrine of humility. Call it what you will. I believe these things to be true, and that they must be said over and over and over, in our schools and libraries and communities; and I say them with all my heart to all Arizonans, New Mexicans, Sonorans, and Southern Californians—Southwesterners, all of us—*mis amigos.*

THE GIFT TO BE SIMPLE

To FIND A TALK to match my title was the problem. The title came easy, two years ago, and since then I have been waiting for the right place to match up a talk to go with it. When the invitation came to address the South Carolina Library Association at Clemson, I knew it was the right place, for the mountains of South Carolina are the Appalachian Mountains, and my title is an Appalachian title. Always conscious of my whereabouts, I would no more think of talking about the Sierra Nevada in South Carolina than I would of trying to sell Los Angeles real estate in San Francisco.

If this was the place for the title, what about the talk? Not easy, even for this man who was born vocal, and has been talking ever since, and especially for the last twenty years of telling the world about the joys of being a librar-

Given at the Annual Conference of the South Carolina Library Association, Clemson, October 27, 1956. First published in Library Journal, *February 1, 1957.*

THE GIFT TO BE SIMPLE

ian. I've never counted the number of talks I have given, seeking only to keep as far as the sound of my voice ahead of my last audience, but it surely runs into the hundreds —and always about our twin stock-in-trade, books and people, playing variations on them, until long ago I ran out of anything new to say. An old family sampler sums up for me the simple good things of life:

> Old wood to burn
> Old wine to drink
> Old books to read
> Old friends to trust

All my life I had been seeking the gift to be simple, but I found it only two and a half years ago, at a time when I was forced to reappraise all I owned. It began with an invitation from Carl White to spend a semester at Columbia, teaching in the library school. I had become critical of library education, and had begun to dream of a new library school at UCLA, and this Columbian invitation was an opportunity to materialize my dreams, and to test my beliefs on students. But as the time neared, I grew nervous. How was I to distill the essences of a lifetime with books, so that students in the course called "Theory of Library Administration" could absorb and be nourished by them? It was imperative that I speak the truth as I saw it, in a way that would carry conviction.

I read and reread much library literature. I sought to determine what I had been doing and why, during the ten years I had been administering a university library; and the more I read and the more I thought, the more troubled

I became. I had been a critic. Now I was to be a library educator. I wished I had never opened my mouth.

Events at Midwinter in Chicago increased my uneasy feelings. There were many meetings and much talk. The weather was cold. It came to be Saturday. My first class was on Monday. I had an inherited syllabus to proceed from. Books were on reserve. Students were poised, with pencil and notebook. And I felt hopeless.

I spent the last evening with a friend whose westbound plane left at midnight, leaving me alone, with three hours to wait for an eastbound flight. If I were a modern Dante, seeking a locale for Inferno, I would choose the Chicago Midway Airport, from midnight to three in the morning, in the dead of winter. I was on emotional dead center, and I just sat there.

The overdue plane finally arrived from San Francisco and Denver, coated with ice, and I trudged through slush, boarded, belted myself in, and slept.

The sun was rising as we landed at La Guardia. It was the miracle of a new day. Coffee! The morning paper! Though Pandora's Box had been opened wide, Hope remained. I went to the King's Crown Hotel and slept till noon. And when I awakened, I reached for the phone, and called my Aunt Mabel, long-time resident of Manhattan.

"What a good time to call," she said. "I have two tickets for the Philharmonic and the friend who was going with me just phoned that she is ill. Meet me at Carnegie Hall."

I did, and we heard music that was good medicine for what ailed me. Mitropoulos conducted Mozart's 29th symphony, a work that speaks sadness and joy, anguish and peace, all in one musical breath—and another composition, which was the one that gave me my title. It was music I had not heard since July 3, 1951, when I had returned from a year in Great Britain and was driving a Hillman all the way West from New York. It was near the end of the first day, and I was somewhere east of Pittsburgh on the Pennsylvania Turnpike, when I turned off into a field, parked, and had my supper of bananas, milk, and fig bars; and over the portable radio I had bought at Macy's, I heard a recording of Aaron Copland's suite from his ballet called *Appalachian Spring*—music that made me as serene as the landscape around me. Parked there in the heart of the Appalachians, surrounded by green trees full of birdsong, it was the perfect time and place to hear such music.

And now three years had passed, and I was hearing it again in Carnegie Hall, and again it had the same effect on me. It spoke to me tenderly, it comforted me as only music can. In the program notes on *Appalachian Spring*, I read that Aaron Copland had taken the final dance melody from an old Shaker song called "Simple Gifts," and the notes gave the words to it, whose first lines are

>'Tis the gift to be simple
>'Tis the gift to be free
>'Tis the gift to come down
>Where we ought to be.

I took those lines to my opening class the next morning, in place of the formal material I had prepared, read them to my thirty-seven students, come together from all over the country and the world, saying, "I'm going to speak to you this semester as simply as I can about what it means to me to be a librarian, to administer libraries, and about what you should know, what you should *be,* if you want to be a good librarian, whether you intend to administer or be administered—for it's just as much of an art to be administered as it is to administer."

The course became one in the simplicities of librarianship, in the elements of our work that do not change, as they relate to administration. I believe these to be: (1) that books are basically useful, that they will be supplemented but not replaced; (2) that people need books and the nourishment they contain; (3) that librarianship consists essentially of collecting and preserving books, and of enabling people to instruct the mind and delight the spirit with books.

A library education should be therefore basically the study of collecting and preserving books and related materials and of serving people with them. Research in librarianship has its place, but let's not believe, as some do, that granting a greenhorn a Ph.D. or a D.L.S. automatically makes him a good librarian. Not even a B.L.S. does this. The education and the discipline of higher degree-taking have their uses, certainly, but it is the *quality* and the *character* of library educators themselves that is more important than all else.

When the social scientists, educationalists, and documentalists entered the book world, they brought their jargon with them. Order and cataloging work became *Technical*

Processes and *Bibliographical Control,* reference work the *Retrieval of Information.* Librarians became *Mediators* in a world of *Spatial Mobility. Communications* became a word as sacrosanct, and meaningless, as *virus* and *allergy.*

All of this they speak of as a revolution, and they patronize the great nineteenth-century librarians for not being scientific researchers. They say our predecessors just guessed the needs of their patrons and the methods by which those needs could be met, often with astonishing accuracy, it is admitted; but, it is stated, this basis for the derivation of library technology is no longer necessary and it should not be perpetuated. This reveals profound contempt for the achievements of our great forerunners—to depreciate their experience, their instinct, and wisdom simply as *guessing.*

In this revolutionary world of the retrievalists, library administration is of course nothing less than a science. Take a young man with some brains and ambition, with an eye to an uncrowded field, and let him study management theory, do some statistical research, and perhaps be what is called an *Interne in Administration,* and then armed with his control span and his chart, let him take over a library and apply scientific management to books and people. Not all such situations result in failure, often for the reason that those unsung heroines, the assistant librarians, usually older women who were passed over for one reason or another, keep the wheels oiled and the pieces picked up.

Librarianship today is suffering from a rash of these brash ones, taught by teachers who have never been successful librarians, or even librarians at all, by researchers who like everything about librarianship except books and the way books have of multiplying, and who would replace books with IBM cards if they could. These inhumanists will do everything to a book but read it. They are in places of power today in library education, and I say they are corrupting the young. I go about a lot and I talk to many librarians, and I find trouble in the land, caused by the maladjustment of these unsocial scientists' graduates. Not only do they not love books, they don't even like them. And people? Irrational beings. Gresham's law operates with librarians as well as with money, and we are seeing bad librarians driving out good.

Any library educator or library administrator whose utterances are devoid of bookish and humane references, is in the wrong work, for books and people are basic in librarianship, and to omit them is to play *Hamlet* without the prince. They believe that the principles of management are universal, and that if a man has managed a shoe-store or a supermarket, he can likewise administer a library. This proves beautifully on paper, for it is true, on paper. But those illogical beings called people are neither fooled nor pleased. The public and the staff know that shoes and groceries and books are different kinds of staples, and that the motivations which bring people into shoe-stores, markets, and libraries, are not the same, and that the satisfactions of the mind and the spirit, which are derived from books, make libraries akin to schools and churches. I have not seen a trend toward recruiting teachers and ministers from the personnel in shoe-stores and supermarkets. To administer libraries calls for gifts of the mind and the spirit, as well as theoretical knowledge of management and knack for gimmicks and gadgets.

I recognize a need for specialists to deal with the proliferation of scientific information. They must be trained to master this material, and therefore schools are needed for their training. Let them be called Documentalists, or Retrievers, or Communicators, or Mass Mediators, rather than Librarians. I have no quarrel with them personally. They are sincere and dedicated men—sincerely wrong and mistakenly dedicated. Humanists need good housekeeping; likewise housekeepers need humanizing.

It is not easy to be simple and to speak basic, bookish English. The line between being simple and being a simpleton is a narrow one. It took me twenty years of librarianship to learn the meaning of these four lines:

> 'Tis the gift to be simple
> 'Tis the gift to be free
> 'Tis the gift to come down
> Where we ought to be.

And when I learned them, my life changed, and I vowed to work until I had seen established a library school based on these simple things, that books are basic, that people are good, and that librarianship is a calling no less dedicated than the ministry or medicine. In our emphasis on the material rewards of library work, we should not overlook the eternal idealism of youth. The discipline of library education should be rigorous, but it must also be idealistic and inspiring, and as imaginative and exciting as library work itself can be. This calls for teaching of the highest creative order. Dullness in teaching is the single deadly sin.

Overloaded curricula now tend to brutalize the student by the sheer mass of data forced on him. The library school experience is regarded by most of the graduates I have employed in the way kids regard a dose of castor oil: hold your nose and get it down, and shun it ever after.

What can be done to improve library education? There are of course many answers. Our answer at UCLA is to plan a new school, in a region of five million people with no publicly supported library school within four hundred miles, and on a campus whose enrollment is now 16,000 but is climbing to an expected 25,000 students within a few years. When they ask us where we would get our students, we reply, primarily from the massive local enrollment. Absence of a library school there now means that each year we are losing forty or fifty future librarians who would be recruited only by the immediate presence of a library school.

Last year twenty members of my staff, with the advice of librarians throughout the Southwest, worked together in blueprinting a new humanistic library school. It was the most exciting and meaningful and believing thing we had ever done. Obstacles were encountered, and we have yet to receive the approval of the University Regents, but we believe in the need for such a school and our belief is widely shared in the profession, and we will see it founded. before much longer.

The school's curriculum will include the three basic

courses I called for in the keynote address at the ALA conference in New York, four years ago.

1. *Introduction to Librarianship,* which will include the history of books and libraries, administration of libraries, and the ethics of our profession.

2. *The Management of Library Materials,* which will include the acquisition, cataloging, care and servicing of books and related items, and of library buildings.

3. *Books and People,* which will include reference, bibliographical, extension, and other services of libraries academic, public, governmental, and special.

There is nothing revolutionary here, except for a rededication to the simple facts of library life. Students should be taught why, how, and for whom, in an atmosphere of intense belief and dedication. "Oh, yes," I hear you say, "all that nonsense will be taken out of them fast on the job."

I say no. Students can also be taught patience. The world will not be reformed overnight, but there *will* be changes made. All change comes from the impact on the many of a few, who believe and who are dedicated to the propagation of their beliefs. This is the kind we will seek to recruit, to educate, and to graduate. Idealistic? Of course it is. Passionately so. And there is a national ground swell rising which will carry us to the goal we seek.

I say again, it is the hardest thing on earth to be simple, to be original, to be imaginative. To be a fool is easy, to imitate is easy, and the line between eloquence and rhetoric is easy to ignore. One of the simplest, most original, imaginative, and eloquent of all Americans was Emerson.

If I had any master for my course at Columbia, it was Emerson. I read from him nearly every time I opened class. Emerson is a dangerous man though, at all times and places, and particularly to teachers who would quote from him, as in this apothegm:

> Do not *say* things. What you *are* stands over you the while and thunders so that I cannot hear what you say to the contrary.

A poem, MacLeish says, should not mean but be. And what of a teacher, who says rather than is? Again let me read Emerson on teachers:

> The teacher should be the complement of the pupil; now, for the most part, they are Earth's diameters wide of each other. A college professor should be elected by setting all the candidates loose on a miscellaneous gang of young men taken at large from the street. He who could get the ear of these youths after a certain number of hours, or of the greatest number of these youths, should be professor.

Why not the same kind of test for library school teachers? Let them compete for the attention of seniors at college commencement, and he who recruits the most to librarianship, let him be professor.

For we need recruits, and once we get them, we need to indoctrinate them with the belief that library work is the best of all work; we need to train them in the ways and means of building and using libraries, in the history of the printed book, and the lives of great bookmen; and we need to set them on fire to go into the field and work, work, work.

The ideals of librarianship are noble, the annals of

librarianship are peopled with great men and women. Library school students should be led to believe in these ideals and to revere these pioneers, and not be graduated, as they often are, cynics and scoffers. To accomplish this act of alchemy, the teachers themselves must be believers, able to articulate and to transmit their beliefs. "Go with mean people," says Emerson, "and you think life is mean."

This might be paraphrased to read, "Listen to dull teachers and you will think librarianship is dull"; then hear such teachers as Althea Warren, Frances Clarke Sayers, and Alice Dugas, and you will wish that the day's work in a library never end, so rich and rewarding is each hour. Fortunately, every library school has had at least one such teaching genius who lives forever in the memory of students.

Let us not teach librarianship as science and technique, or load the curriculum with drill and drudgery. Rather should it be taught as a humane calling of service to people. In the beginning the *why* of librarianship is more important than the *how*. After philosophical orientation, students should also learn the tactile joys of handling books, of the sight and the smell and the feel of books, new and old, of how to work a nail-puller, dress an exhibit case, maneuver a loaded book-truck. There is a fine art to these simple things, and the librarian who has not mastered them, to use whenever necessary, is not a good librarian, even though his span of control be as wide as the Golden Gate Bridge, or as narrow as Chancery Lane. The theory and the practice of librarianship are constantly diverging. The good librarian must be able to shift back and forth between them in the course of the day's work, must be like a circus rider with his feet on two horses.

One theory of librarianship says that some things are professional, some things are clerical, and never the twain should meet. I am glad I went to a library school where the differences were not emphasized, for if I had come to my beginning job at UCLA with my hands in gloves and my eyes glued to the chart on the wall, I would not be doing what I am today. One Saturday afternoon during my first year, when I was the skeleton crew in the order department, an older faculty man came in, spotted me at my desk where I was carding a truck, and called, "Boy, come unload my car."

"What's in it?" I parried.

"Books," he said, already walking off, assuming that I was following.

If he had said shoes or slide rules, I would have probably told him, politely of course, to go to hell, that I was a professional librarian not hired to do manual labor. But *books*—they were irresistible.

I followed that professor to the loading dock, flattered, I suppose, at being taken for a student, but also suffering from a lifelong curiosity about all books not yet seen and handled. I unloaded his car, without bothering to introduce myself, and I did not see him face to face for six years, until we met again, he on the President's committee to select a new university librarian, I as a candidate, appearing for interview. He gave no sign of remembering our first meeting, but I learned later that when he cast his vote in my favor, he said cryptically, "He can carry his weight in books."

I realize that I am sinning, in the New England sense, by being personal, but I come from the far corner, and Southern Californians may suffer from smog, but not from reticence.

One final example, again from my own experience, is about the theory and practice of administration. Thou shalt delegate, commands the syllabus, and in theory it is good doctrine, but one must not be bound by it. A leader in the community died last year, and left his books and papers to UCLA; and after an interval his widow phoned me and said the materials were ready to be picked up, in fact needed to be removed that very morning. I was in a critical meeting, and suggested that the new man in the order department come for the gift. There was a moment of silence, and then the widow said, timidly, "Dr. Powell, would you mind coming too. There are some things I want to give into your own hands."

So I left what I was doing, and the junior staff member and I went off in a truck to make the pickup. It was a hot day. The house was a two-storied one, packed with a lifetime of collecting. We made many trips up and down stairs, going from room to room, with the lady at our sides, speaking of this book and that carton of papers, with tears in her eyes, as her half century of marriage was evoked by the things she was giving to us.

My colleague and I really had a wonderful time, as our sweat dripped and our shirts wilted, for this was an ancient rite of librarianship we were performing. We were the human links in the transmission of recorded knowledge and history, from a leader in the region to the library fitted to be a repository for such archives. Here was the practice of librarianship in one of its most basic and simple forms. Loading books and papers into a truck can be a clerical task, but it can also be a divine duty. Beware of those who deny the truth of biblio-osmosis, the absorption of knowledge by the laying of hands on books.

Human values and human judgments are inseparable from good librarianship. They should be woven into every hour of instruction in every course in every library school; and to do this calls for inspired teaching by humanists who have been seasoned and humbled and made simple by living with books, by working with people, and loving both. Salaries and certification, the classification of jobs, and the co-ordination of curricula, are all important, and must be dealt with, but beneath these complexities lie the great simplicities of humane librarianship—that books are basic, that people are good, and that bringing the two together, so that books are made more useful and people more fruitful, is one of the most exciting and rewarding experiences on earth. It is called librarianship.

And this is what I came here to say to you, and am going to say elsewhere, as long as I live and wherever I go, be it in the Appalachians, the Sangres, the Tehachapis, or the Catalinas. Of all the diversity of gifts bestowed by the Lord on his children, the one to seek and the one to cherish is

> The gift to be simple,
> The gift to be free,
> The gift to come down
> Where we ought to be.

FROM PRIVATE COLLECTION
TO PUBLIC INSTITUTION

THE FATE OF A MAN'S BOOKS after his death sooner or later troubles every collector. What will become of those scores or hundreds or thousands of volumes which during the years of his life gave him instruction, delight, distraction, and solace? Should they be left to wife or children, or be sold for their benefit, or be willed to an institution? Quoting Edmond de Goncourt in justification, A. Edward Newton ordered his books dispersed, so that other collectors now and in years to come might have the pleasure of re-collecting them, and so that they "shall not be consigned to the cold tomb of a museum, and subjected to the stupid glance of the careless passer-by."

There are dangers in making an unrestricted gift of books to a library; for Randolph G. Adams was right: librarians are too often among the enemies of books. Only the wealthiest of collectors, such as Huntington, Folger,

First published in Library Quarterly, *April 1950.*

Morgan, Clements, or Clark, can insure the security of their gifts by providing separate buildings and, usually, endowments. Few impecunious collectors could achieve the witty triumph of Samuel Pepys in achieving the perpetual integrity of his collection—without cost to himself. Only two weeks before his death, in the spring of 1703, Pepys added a second codicil to his will, beginning:

> I do hereby declare That could I be sure of a constant Succession of Heirs from my said nephew qualified like himself for the use of such a Library I should not entertain a thought of its ever being Alienated from them. But this uncertainty considered with the infinite paines and time and cost employed in my Collecting Methodizing and reducing the same to the State wherein it now is I cannot but be greatly Solicitous that all possible provision should be made for its unalterable preservation and perpetual Security against the ordinary fate of such Collections falling into the hands of an incompetent heir and thereby of being sold dissipated or imbezelled.

The testator therefore proceeds to state his "present thoughts and prevailing inclinations" in this matter, as follows:

> 1st That after the death of my said nephew my said Library be placed and for ever Settled in one of our Universities and rather in that of Cambridge than Oxford. 2dly And rather in a private College there than the publick Library. 3dly And in the College of Trinity or Magdalen preferable to All others. 4thly And of these two Caeteris paribus, rather in the latter for the Sake of my own and nephews Education therein. 5thly That in

which soever of the two it is a faire roome be provided therein on purpose for it and wholly and soly appropriated thereto. 6thly And if in Trinity, That the said room be contiguous to and have Communication with the new Library there. 7thly And if in Magdalen That it be in the new building there, and any part thereof at my nephews Election. 8thly That my said Library be continued in its present form and noe other books mixt therewith Save what my Nephew may add to them of his own Collection in distinct presses. 9thly That the said roome and books so placed and adjusted be called by the name of Bibliotheca Pepysiana. 10thly That this Bibliotheca Pepysiana be under the sole power and custody of the Master of the College for the time being who shall neither himself convey nor Suffer to be conveyed by others any of the said books from thence to any other place except to his own Lodge in the said College nor there have more than ten of them at a time and that of those also a strict entry be made and account kept of the time of their having been taken out and returned, in a booke to be provided and remain in the said Library for that only purpose. 11thly That before my said Library be put into the possession of either of the said Colleges, that College for which it shall be designed first enter into Covenants for performance of the foregoing articles. 12thly And that for a yet further Security herein the said two Colleges of Trinity and Magdalen have a Reciprocal Check upon one another. And that the College which shall be in present possession of the said Library be subject to an Annual visitation from the other and to the forfeiture thereof to the like possession and Use of the other upon Conviction of any breach of their said Covenants.

William Andrews Clark, Jr., was not an impecunious book collector; nor was he a Croesus. The fingers of two hands would more than number his millions, and, at his death in 1934, he left a library of only sixteen thousand volumes. By willing his private collection, complete with building and grounds, to a public institution—the University of California at Los Angeles—Clark joined the select company of American book collectors whose bequests are among the glories of our national library strength. Clark's request was neither casual nor crotchety. The gift deed was executed in 1926, eight years before his death, and reserved to the donor during his lifetime the full use of the Library and property. Since 1934 the University has maintained and developed the Clark Library in accordance with the gift deed, and it is my purpose in this paper to scrutinize the subsequent record and to note the way in which a private collection with several highly specialized segments has been transformed into a public institution.

It should be said, first of all, that W. A. Clark, Jr., was a book collector by instinct, not merely by virtue of his wealth. He was a reader as well as a collector of books. He was also generous by nature and not solely for benefit of tax deductions. The memorial library to his father, the Montana senator, which is UCLA's richest single endowment, was only one of his benefactions, which included also a law school building to his alma mater, the University of Virginia, in memory of his first wife; Poe and Jefferson manuscripts to the Alderman Library at Virginia; a library building to the University of Nevada in memory of his second wife; and the founding of a symphony orchestra in the city of Los Angeles.

The family fortune was made in Montana copper, and Senator Clark spent no small part of it on the art objects in his Fifth Avenue mansion, which were willed by him to the Corcoran Gallery. His other son, Charles, was also a collector of books, notably early printing, and the catalog of his library, printed by John Henry Nash in 1914-22, is a distinguished collection's only memorial; for the Charles Clark books were left to his family and have been dispersed by sale.

In 1909 Will Clark, settled in the then fashionable West Adams district of Los Angeles, began collecting English literature so earnestly that in a little more than a decade he found it necessary to employ two librarians, Robert Ernest Cowan and Cora Edgerton Sanders. In 1920 appeared the first volume of the catalog of his library, which, over the next ten years, grew to a total of twenty volumes. Clark's preface to this volume seems to me worth quoting in part for the unconscious portrait it gives of a modest man who loved books more than he loved himself:

> If it is axiomatic that every book should have a preface, then *a fortiori,* a book about books should therewith be the more necessarily adorned. I shall not, as so many others have done, proffer as an excuse for the publication of this volume, that I have been urged to do so by my friends. In truth I find but few persons that are really interested in old and rare books and in the first editions with their variations.

As I became interested in rare books and in their acquisition, I naturally turned to the study of bibliographies, but having in the course of a few idle months made copious notes on the volumes that I had collected, it occurred to me to put these notes into a permanent form by publishing them in a printed catalogue. From the various catalogues of other libraries that I had carefully studied, I culled from each what in my judgment were the best and most essential features of compilation and collation, resulting in the scheme herein presented. For this purpose it required a complete revision of what data I had gathered together, a task for which I had not the time, owing to many business interests that required attention, to undertake myself.

Fortunately I was able to call to my assistance Mr. Robert Ernest Cowan of San Francisco, a man of most profound scholarly attainments, a bibliographer well known to book lovers, and a gentleman in the true sense of the word, with whom it was a pleasure to collaborate whenever I could spare the time from my other occupations. I had personally collated a great part of this volume, which he carefully checked over and corrected in many details. Many of the volumes we collated together, many he collated personally, so that all in all the work may be called the result of our joint efforts. I shall always hold in fondest memory the many pleasant hours that we passed together in my modest library at Los Angeles. To Miss Cora Edgerton Sanders of Los Angeles, I wish to express my thanks for her valuable assistance to us in our work. . . .

I claim no originality in research, but have combined in this volume so far as I could all the information of interest that is scattered through many printed catalogues and bibliographies, which I trust may make the book one of value for those who are not fortunate enough to possess the works cited in the references. Mistakes no doubt have been made, and I would be grateful to have these pointed out to me as they are discovered.

The relation of Will Clark with his printer, John Henry Nash, is worthy of study. In addition to the catalog, Clark commissioned Nash to print for private distribution the well-known series of Christmas books—facsimiles of such treasures in the Clark Library as *Tamerlane* and *Adonais*, accompanied by sumptuous modern reprints. The Nash Papers in the University Library at Berkeley and in the Clark Memorial Library are primary sources for such a study.

In 1923 a fire in the Clark residence frightened the collector, and led him to commission architect Robert D. Farquhar to plan a separate, fireproof building. The structure cost $750,000 and is a jeweled oasis in a desert of stucco.

In planning the Library, Clark had not decided that it was eventually to be a public institution, and so the functional idea of public service was not uppermost in mind (as it was, for example, in the planning of the Houghton Library). In the Clark Library, rare books have the rooms of honor on the main floor; readers are relegated to the basement. And thus, upon taking possession in 1934, the University had the twofold problem of how to adapt the building to public use and of what collections to develop.

In Regent Edward A. Dickson, President Robert Gordon Sproul, and Provost Ernest Carroll Moore the University had three top officials who were appreciative of the material value of the bequest and sensitive to the donor's wishes. It is worth repeating that Clark's deed or gift was neither careless nor crippling. The Library was not to be merged or consolidated with any other institution. The books were never to be removed from the building, nor were they ever to be "perforated or otherwise disfigured." In so stipulating, Clark had not forgotten his experience when, several years before, in visiting another local institution (a possible recipient of the bequest before it had been made to the state university), he saw copies of his privately printed Christmas books, which he had given to that institution, perforated, stamped, and inked with call numbers on the backstrips.

Clark's stated object in giving the books, building, and grounds was "the advancement of learning, the arts and sciences, and to promote the public welfare." The administration, management, maintenance, and development of the Library was left to the discretion of the Regents of the University. As their executive officer, President Sproul appointed a library committee, with himself as chairman, which included the provost of the University at Los Angeles, the University librarian at Los Angeles, and several members of the faculty; the first three were members ex officio, the latter were subject each year to reappointment or replacement.

The second wise step was the appointment of Cora Edgerton Sanders, long-time librarian to Clark, as curator of the Memorial Library; and her familiarity with the Library's contents, her bibliophilic sophistication, and her innate good taste were invaluable to the Library until her retirement from state service, in 1944, at the compulsory age.

From 1934 to 1938 the program for the Clark Library received intensive study by the committee. A reading of the minutes shows how conscientiously the University sought to carry out the letter and the spirit of Clark's bequest; and it was Miss Sanders who was able to read between the lines of the gift deed and recall from conversations what was in Clark's mind when he wrote them.

Several projects were advanced from within and without the University for the expenditure of income from the $1,500,000 endowment, after the necessary grounds and building maintenance expenses were met. But in the end it was agreed that the collections must be broadened and deepened if the Library was to attain true research strength and usefulness.

But which collections? Shakespeare and the Renaissance? Dryden and the Restoration? French dramatists of the late seventeenth century? The English Romantic poets? Oscar Wilde and his contemporaries? Montana history? Printing and bibliography? In all of these disparate areas the Library had starts ranging from good to excellent.

While it was true that the Library contained an impressive group of folios and quartos, as well as certain rare works of Shakespeare's contemporaries, the pre-1641 holdings were not to be ranked with the English Renaissance collection in the Henry E. Huntington Library. And in the field of early printing, again, the Clark's few incunabula were dwarfed by the Huntington's massive holdings. Thus the idea of regional co-operation was accepted from the beginning, and the Clark has refrained from collecting in the earlier period.

As for the French dramatists, Clark's early schooling and later travels in France had given him an abiding love for that country, and he had acquired a superlative collection of first editions of Corneille, Racine, Molière, and Lesage. This is an expensive field, in which the purchase of one or two dozen books could use up the Library's entire book fund of a given year, as well as a field in which UCLA scholars were not actively engaged; and so it was decided to let the French collection remain dormant.

A comparison of the Dryden collection with that of the English Romantics showed the seventeenth century by far the stronger. The book fund was not large enough to develop both, and so a decision was made in favor of the earlier period.

As for the Oscar Wilde collection, so complete was it in original works and Wildeana that little could be added apart from occasional manuscripts and letters, new editions and reprints, and contemporary publishing on Wilde. Montana history was likewise represented by a strong collection, but it did not truly represent Clark's interest. In spite of his Montana origin, Clark's collection on his native state was the result not of his own but of his librarian's enthusiasm for Western Americana. The de-

PRIVATE COLLECTION TO PUBLIC INSTITUTION 195

cision was to leave this general field to the University library, which, in 1936, acquired Robert E. Cowan's own distinguished library of Californiana.

A good start had been made by Clark in collecting bibliographical works, particularly on English literature, printing, and publishing, and this was continued. As for reference works, a selective policy was adopted which would bring in the standard biographies and modern critical editions of the English literary figures from 1651 to 1750. The Library's distance of ten miles from the campus required a certain amount of duplication of holdings in the University library, but shortage of funds, of shelf space, and of staff were primary reasons for the Clark's decision not to assemble a complete reference library on its specialty periods in the way that the comparatively isolated Huntington Library was compelled to do. Although Clark books could not be taken to the campus, the University library's volumes could be readily charged to scholars working intensively at the West Adams location.

Thus the Library's development has been dictated by the proximity of two strong research libraries, the Huntington and the UCLA; and, from 1943 until Louis B. Wright's departure to the Folger Library, the Clark committee included faculty representatives who held joint appointments in the UCLA English department and on the Huntington staff. Since his appointment as Folger director, Dr. Wright has continued to serve on the Clark's advisory committee.

Since 1934 the Library has grown from sixteen thousand volumes to more than sixty thousand, and most of the accessions have been in the 1641-1750 period. It has been estimated that English publishing during those hundred years totaled three hundred thousand items, an essential collection of which might reach one third of that number.

The Clark Library is acquiring books in virtually all branches of English culture, including literature, philosophy, religion and science, economics, geography, and history. The emphasis has been on acquiring many inexpensive and moderately priced items rather than a few costly "high spots," with which the Library was already rather well endowed.

Publication of Wing's *Short-Title Catalogue . . . 1641-1700* has been both a boon and a bane to collectors. The only negative result has been to raise prices. On the affirmative side, libraries can now learn what there is to be collected and the location of items in other libraries. Wing's prefatory proviso should not be overlooked: "This is not a census of copies, but rather an effort to locate copies available in various geographical sections. Normally, therefore, not more than one copy is listed in the same city." The compiler's apparent unfamiliarity with Western geography led him repeatedly to cite the Huntington copy of a given book rather than the Clark, although the two libraries are in widely different parts of a metropolitan area which is itself larger than some of the Eastern states.

The curator's retirement, in 1944, was followed by the appointment of a director who also became librarian of the University library. Even closer co-operation between the Clark and the University library was thus assured. An

PRIVATE COLLECTION TO PUBLIC INSTITUTION

intensive review of the Clark program resulted in no change in the basic collecting policy, although it was extended to include local fine printing, virtually all the examples of which come as gifts.

The Library's sphere of activity was enlarged. A program was undertaken to publish through the University Press certain unique materials in the Library, edited by faculty scholars. A project to re-edit Dryden's works, which had been suspended because of the war, was reactivated, and the first of what may run to a twenty-volume subscription set appeared in 1956. A similar project on Oscar Wilde has been considered, and a catalog of Wilde and Wildeana manuscripts was issued in 1957. The Library prepares an occasional acquisitions bulletin called *Mercurius Redivivus*. In 1949 the Library assumed responsibility for publishing the "Augustan Reprints," a series founded by Professors E. N. Hooker and H. T. Swedenberg of UCLA and R. C. Boys of Michigan to make cheaply available to scholars and libraries photographic facsimiles of seventeenth- and eighteenth-century works. A member of the library staff was added to the editorial board.

Other than a drawing room, in which only a small number of folding chairs can be placed, the Library has no facility for large meetings. An open-house Founder's Day celebration has been held periodically since 1945 in honor of the donor. Friends in the University and the community are welcomed, and are instructed by exhibits and talks and regaled with an outdoor presentation, by student and faculty performers, of some dramatic or musical offering drawn from materials in the Library. In the course of these celebrations, the Library produced Coffey's ballad-opera, *The Devil to Pay,* the Dryden-Handel *Alexander's Feast,* Dryden's *Marriage à la Mode,* Shakespeare's *A Midsummer Night's Dream,* scenes from *The Beggar's Opera,* folk dances from Playford's *English Dancing Master,* Wilde's *The Importance of Being Earnest,* and, in the Gold Rush year, a rousing revival of the melodrama known as *A Live Woman in the Mines.* In 1953 the Library observed the two hundred fiftieth anniversary of the death of Samuel Pepys, whose works and memorabilia are present in large numbers.

Throughout the University's administration of the Library the faculty has made increasing use of the Library's facilities by holding seminars in the rare-book rooms. Under gentle supervision, students in English literature, history, philosophy, theater arts, music, history of science, fine printing, and bibliography gain the stimulation of firsthand experience with the printed records of the periods and subjects of their study. To hold in hand (and students are taught *how* to hold and handle rare books) a Milton, a Dryden, a Purcell, or a Newton first edition, in original seventeenth-century binding, is an experience not available to most students, not even at the Huntington Library, where because of heavy usage, only advanced scholars have access to rare books.

The civilizing effect of fine libraries and rare books is a real one, particularly in the Far West, where such centers are uncommon in a comparatively bookless land. Will Clark left his library intentionally to the state university,

PRIVATE COLLECTION TO PUBLIC INSTITUTION 199

for he believed in democratic education and was aware of the potential role of rare books in this process. He would have been pleased by the reaction of one seminar student who attended the first session wearing a shabby suit and no necktie. After a tour through the beautiful building and a two-hour session in the bronze-cased book room, surrounded by ten thousand rare volumes, he returned the following week still wearing the shabby suit (probably his only one) but with shoes shined and a necktie.

The Clark Library is not able to serve masses of people, but from the masses who throng the state university it can magnetize to it the few who can be educated beyond the average and upon whom the transmission of culture depends. This is a Jeffersonian concept with which Clark became familiar while he was a student at the University of Virginia.

The Library also aids research by offering an annual graduate fellowship to a UCLA student who has particular need of Clark materials to complete his dissertation.

In 1953 the Library instituted an annual invitational seminar, led by two scholars in chosen fields of the Library's strength and attended by fifty scholars from California universities and colleges, and later publishing the proceedings for free distribution to scholars everywhere.

A separate paper could be written about the organization, the staffwork, and the technical processes of the Library, for it is on their smooth and efficient functioning that the collecting and service policies of the Library depend. Much thought, experiment, trial, and error have gone into simplifying these routines. Cataloging is neither full-dress bibliographical description nor simplified cataloging but a middle course which registers the pertinent information and locates the book. Main cards go also to the UCLA catalog and to the union catalogs in the University library at Berkeley and the Library of Congress.

The staff includes two librarians, two clerical aids, a custodian, and two gardeners. A bindery was established in garage quarters formerly occupied by servants, to repair, reback, and rebind leather books and to make cloth cases and portfolios for fragile items and heavy paper cases for the pamphlet collection. Leather-bound volumes are oil-dressed and polished, and a regular program is followed of re-oiling older books, cleaning the shelves, and fumigating the entire building. The regional problem in the care of rare books is dryness and dust rather than dampness and mold. Maintenance of the grounds and building is the responsibility of the University superintendent, all expenses being met from the endowment income. The director's executive officer in charge of the Library is known as the "supervising bibliographer"—with equal emphasis on "administrator and bookman"—and H. Richard Archer was the incumbent from 1944 to 1952, succeeded by William E. Conway. Microfilming is done by the University library's photographic division.

The Library's greatest problem rapidly became that of expansion for books and readers. Each year between fifteen hundred and two thousand volumes are added, and, as the collections grow, more readers are attracted. In addition to the increase in research by UCLA faculty and students, more and more scholars at the Huntington

Library have found it worth while to investigate the Clark's holdings. Every available space was filled with books, until the saturation point was reached. In addition to stacks, the need was for studies and cubicles where advanced scholars might pursue their work without distraction by visitors and by others working in the reading room.

Both needs were met in 1951 by the construction of an underground annex, connected by passageway with the basement reading room. Storage space thus gained will not be filled for an estimated twenty-five years, at which time, thanks to the large lawn adjoining the building, another underground unit can be added, and so on and on. This type of buried construction is the most economical to build, to maintain, and to enlarge, and it also affords better security in time of war.

Such, then, are the bare facts of the transformation of the Clark Library from private collection to public institution. Those who knew Will Clark and heard him voice his hopes for the future of his library say that the transformation has richly realized these hopes. The building and grounds are in immaculate condition, the books are zealously conserved and carefully used, the collections multiply and are made known; and from many cities, states, and countries earnest men and women come to study the printed legacy of the past. Although it is composed of so-called "dead" things—books, wood, metal, and stone —the Library is a living organism, not the "cold tomb of a museum" abhorred by Goncourt and Newton. The University of California proudly treasures the Clark Library; and, at the same time, it modestly hopes that its stewardship thereof will help allay the fears of collectors for the future of their books and encourage them to do like Sam Pepys or Will Clark, whose private collections, by one means and another, were successfully transformed into public institutions.

BOOKS WILL BE READ

SIMPLE STATEMENT OF BELIEF, employing basic English. Articles of faith. A credo. Not a learned lecture, or a dissertation; not the abstract of a research project, or the summary of a questionnaire. When I applied to the research committee of my university for travel money to fly me all the way to Yorkshire, from the farthest southwestern corner of the United States, all I could offer was a title, "Books Will Be Read," and a statement that the lecture would contain the essence of my twenty years as a librarian. Their answer was short: what you propose is not a research lecture—application denied.*

I did not argue. I do not have much respect for research in librarianship, or for the Ph.D. program in American library schools—at least not as preparation for library

Annual Lecture, The Library Association, Great Britain, 1957.
* The University generously provided other funds.

administration, as it is usually regarded. Taking a research degree no more fits one to be a librarian than it does to be a teacher. What librarianship needs is to recruit and to fit young men and women for basic librarianship—librarians who will do well, because they believe in what they are doing. Believers and doers are what we need—faithful librarians who are humble in the presence of books. To enter a library, no matter its kind or size, is to enter the heart of the whirlwind. To be in a library is one of the purest of all experiences. This awareness of a library's unique, even sacred nature is what should be instilled in our neophytes. The absence of this basic motivation to teach librarianship in moral, even religious terms, as a calling and a dedicated way of life, is what I most deplore in today's library education.

This preamble is meant to put me on record, to lay a foundation for my lecture, for I believe that one of the themes this week is Library Education. Those who came to hear a discourse by an academician may leave now, with no hard feelings on my part. It may seem silly to have asked a librarian to come overseas simply to say what some of the most literate librarians on earth know so well that it is taken for granted. Books will be read? It is like saying there will always be an England. Of course, and so what? The truth is I love this ancestral island, and Normandy, whence my people also came, and deeper Burgundy, where I went to school; and I love books—by, on, and for which I live. And like to talk, of course, to share the riches life has given me. And so for these reasons I came, and am glad I did.

For I didn't see enough of librarians seven years ago, when I was here on sabbatical leave. Instead I spent most of that year in bookshops, acquiring research items for my young library, so greatly in need of all manner of scholarly materials; and on the highways and byways, in cafés and cathedrals, seeking the essences of Britain. And finding such a richness of history and humanity to last the rest of my life, if necessary.

This made easy a return to Britain, plus a lifelong passion for travel. This I owe to a book. A book of poems which my mother knew by heart, and which I was always begging her to recite to me. That and *Grimms' Fairy Tales* were *the* books of my childhood. What is the book of poems? It is by a Scot who passed through California, en route to his rendezvous with death in Samoa. The poem called "Travel" from *A Child's Garden of Verses* was, I think, the most determining piece of literature in my life, and is probably why I am here today, in the lee of Hadrian's Wall, with Auld Reeky like a magnet in the north. Recall its opening lines:

> I should like to rise and go
> Where the golden apples grow;—

And its closing lines:

> There I'll come when I'm a man
> With a camel caravan;
> Light a fire in the gloom
> Of some dusty dining room;
> See the pictures on the walls,
> Heroes, fights and festivals;

And in a corner find the toys
Of the old Egyptian boys.

And I did go to Egypt, in my nineteenth year, as musician on a round-the-world liner, and to other exotic countries, to the simple rhythms of this single travel poem by an equally foot-loose Scot. And this is a good way to live, with life and literature wedded in equal partnership.

My thesis is that books will always be read by people. as long as there are books and people, and in spite of librarians. I am not worried, for I have observed people reading books under all kinds of circumstances, all over the world, and without help from librarians. In *The Anatomy of Bibliomania* there is a chapter on Readers and Their Reading Places, which tells of a learned German in Athens who was supposed to have a Homer printed on India rubber, to read during his bath.

The presence of paperback books in all countries, and in the United States in such unlikely places as drugstores and supermarkets, has been a great boon for readers. TV has not lessened reading, any more than movies or the automobile did. The desire to read is nearly as deep as the desire for food and love.

It is almost as much pleasure to observe its gratification as it is to read. On that round-the-world voyage, we musicians bunked below with the engineers. The refrigeration engineer was a Nordic who spoke sub-basic English. He was trying to learn more by reading. His unlikely text was *Jean Christophe* in English translation. He spent his off-shift time in his bunk, puzzling through Romain

Rolland's masterpiece, calling on me to help him through the labyrinthine passages, to the music of the engine room and the master smell of oil-hot machinery. A few years later when I was a student at the University of Dijon, I used to visit the nearby hill village of Vézelay, from whose Romanesque basilica St. Bernard preached the Second Crusade. One day while toiling up the narrow street to the church, I saw an elderly man reading in a garden, seated under a flowering chestnut tree—Yeats's "great-rooted blossomer." He was pointed out to me as Romain Rolland. I longed to speak to him, yet I never did. The emotion I felt merely in seeing him and recalling my associations with his *Jean Christophe* was all the purer for not involving his personality.

Another time I remember taking our sons to a neighborhood carnival when they were little, and giving them rides on the merry-go-round. The ticket seller was a fat woman of no visible beauty. She was reading a book, as she sold tickets. I maneuvered into position, from where I could see what she was reading. It was Colette's delicate love story called *Chéri*.

Now our sons are grown and married, and we live in the country, on the ocean's edge, thirty miles from campus. Last summer, a city family rented the house next to us, and their four daughters, ranging from seventeen to nine, spent the days on the beach, sunning and bathing, playing and reading. Yes, *reading*, all four of them, lying on their stomachs, reading the *Odyssey, Ivanhoe, Huckleberry Finn,* and *Punda, the Tiger Horse* (a zebra, of course). I made the mistake of asking the girls where they had obtained these books, for their swift answer was scornful of my ignorance.

"From the Bookmobile, of course!" meaning the Malibu Bookmobile of the Los Angeles County Public Library, serving a territory of 3,300 square miles, which came once a week with Homer, Scott, and Mark Twain, even down to the sands of the sea, bringing "tales which holdeth children from play and old men from the chimney corner."

One of the joys of my middle-age has been in reading the book called *Islandia*, a vast Utopian novel written secretly by an American professor of admiralty law, and published posthumously in 1942. I have talked much about this masterpiece by Austin T. Wright, even written an essay about it; and everywhere I have talked, in many parts of the United States and to all kinds of audiences, there was always at least one person present who had read the book and was thereby a fellow Islandian, and who came forward afterward to speak the language of that faraway country. One young man said he had found the volume on the bookshelf of his aunt, during a boyhood visit to her ranch in the White Mountains of Arizona, and that he subsequently read it four times before he left his teens. Another time a woman told me that she had learned about it in a letter from her son, who was serving on a submarine in the Pacific during World War II, where he had found the book in the ship's library. Soon after his letter came, she was informed by the Secretary of the Navy that her son had been lost, when the submarine and all aboard had presumably been sunk by enemy action. Now she reads *Islandia* once a year, in memory of her boy.

Books will be read? Of course they will, forever and always, regardless of how remote from books we librarians become, as a result of bad leadership in recent years, which has led us after the false gods of housekeeping into the desert of jargon. Talking about techniques has become for many a substitute for reading. Too busy to read, they say. Fatal admission, I say, made by those who thereby disqualify themselves as librarians. There is no substitute for reading. Certainly not talking about books, or listening to talkers.

I used to be in demand as a speaker at the dedication of library buildings, until I said that the building is the least important factor in a library situation, occupying last place after books and staff.

Books are of course the most important, for a roomful of books, without any attendant, to which knowing readers have access, *is* a library. But when there is more than a roomful, when there are stacks of books in the complex arrangement of a great public or research library, then the people in charge, those with the keys, are gods indeed. And if the prospective reader is unknowing and in need of help and the librarians are unreading, unwilling, gadgety, and ambitious only for self-advancement through the fringes of benefit to the throne of administration, then pity the poor reader—he is better off in drugstore and supermarket.

What I am saying is that the two chief attributes of a good librarian are that he be a reader of books, and a servant of those in need of help. These two things are born in people, and can be encouraged and stimulated, educated and disciplined. Given these two motivations in a young person, all the rest of the housekeeping operations can be taught, in schools and on the job. Give me young library school graduates who come to their first jobs long on enthusiasm and belief and short on housekeeping techniques. They can be quickly taught the latter in the course of their work, for enthusiasm makes learning swift and easy. But if they are graduated as cynical and unbelieving technicians, ambitious for a quick climb to the top of the ladder, nothing can be done to reform them.

The trouble is, the schools are admitting students without these two basic attributes of eagerness to read and desire to serve readers. I do not like some of the questionnaires they send out to persons whom the candidate has given as references. They are often long forms, with a list of qualities to check in places marked *superior, above average, good, fair,* etc.

My idea of a form is simpler. I would ask only three questions:

Does the candidate read books?
Does he like to serve people?
Has he the ability to study and to learn?

Such a student can be imbued with belief in the opportunities and the challenges of librarianship as a dedicated way of life, only if his teachers are believers. From the present literature of library education one gets the impression that the teachers are more concerned with the degree structure, technicalities of credits and curricula, and with such questions as to whether or not a library school Dean should also hold the position of Librarian.

The fact that American librarianship has been dominated in recent years by those who have no real interest in books is reflected also in the present pattern of American library associations, organizations, and conferences, which have become deserts of bureaucratic shoptalk, of housekeeping business, and of the proliferation of committees, to such a degree as to take the heart out of librarians who, if they persist in attending national conferences, wander about in search of bookish spokesmen and leaders.

When Patricia Paylore, president of the Southwestern Library Association, representing Louisiana, Texas, Arkansas, Oklahoma, New Mexico, and Arizona, published in the *Wilson Library Bulletin* her presidential address called "The Heart of the Matter," in which she deplored the absence of bookish and humane programs of instruction in many American library schools, the response from readers filled columns of subsequent issues of that periodical. From all parts of the land, from all kinds of librarians in varied libraries, came a rising *Amen*, indicating to me that American librarianship, as represented by many of its administrators and library educators, is out of touch with the deepest needs of the rank and file.

If the trend toward bureaucratization and mechanization continues, I predict a revolution, not by librarians, but by readers—townspeople, students, and teachers—those who use the library in their need for knowledge and delight, who think of the library as a kind of temple, and who sicken of social scientists and personnel psychologists, of documentalists and gadgeteers, in places of power. These good people, who expect libraries to be manned by librarians, will invade the libraries one fine day and drive the pretenders into the streets, saying, "If you choose to worship false gods, do it elsewhere, not in the libraries." They will take it upon themselves to operate the libraries in the way they were operated in the good old days, with simple belief, faith, and joy, and with these words over the doorway:

"Have as few rules as possible, and break them all whenever necessary."

The handwriting is there. More and more nonlibrarians are being appointed to high posts by executives who do not like what they see passing for librarians. There is also a trend toward taking top library administrators out of their posts and making them some other kind of administrator—which seems to me an admission that the person had been in the wrong work all his life. I will not admit any calling, other than the ministry and medicine, higher than that of librarianship, when practiced at its best.

There is a belief that the principles of management, whether applied to librarianship, banking, or undertaking, can be taught without reference to what the principles are to be applied to. Take books out of library education, and what's left is a puppet show called human engineering.

This has been a jeremiad, and it may have been the wrong kind of lecture, perhaps unexpected from a son of the Golden West, where the people are legendarily optimistic; and yet even more unpalatable, I am sure, would be a panegyric of American librarianship. Then why not a discourse on British librarianship from an American viewpoint? Because I do not know enough firsthand about British libraries. I have read about them, past and present, but that is not enough. Books will be read, yes, and also life will be lived—and life comes first—life in which books are as basic as food and air.

I can speak at firsthand about American libraries, all kinds, in all parts of the United States, for I am a tireless traveler and library visitor. Wherever I am, I make for the nearest library to see how it goes with them, and also to get my hands on books. I am a believer in the tactile, as well as the visual joys of librarianship. I like the feel of books, as well as the feelings books engender.

During recent years, in addition to libraries in my homeland of California, I have been in libraries in New York, the District of Columbia, the Carolinas, Alabama, Maryland, Tennessee, Georgia, Louisiana, Missouri, Kansas, Pennsylvania, Massachusetts, Connecticut, Rhode Island, New Jersey, Indiana, Michigan, Wisconsin, Illinois, Texas, Arizona, and New Mexico. I have spoken to and heard from librarians and users of libraries in all these far-flung places, finding myself linked with them all as readers of books.

Those who have traveled in the United States since the last war appreciate the enormous differences between, say, Boston and El Paso: differences of climate, vegetation, architecture, dress, and all the rhythms of living. In appearance no two public library buildings could be more different, the one as monumentally noble (and rigid) as New England itself; the other a down-to-earth Southwestern structure, adobe-colored, and decorated by Tom

Lea, equally well-adapted to the character of this border town, where the Rio Grande flows between Texas and Mexico.

Enormous differences, I said; superficial differences, I add. For the motives of a New Englander and of a Southwesterner, in entering the public libraries of Boston and El Paso, are identical. He wants to know and to learn, to confirm or deny, test or prove, to merge with or escape from life; and whatever his motive or his need, it will be recognized and satisfied, in no matter what library he enters, in what city, state, or country, if books are still basic in that library. For the book is the common key to the mind and heart, no matter the language in which it is printed, and readers and librarians are a universal brotherhood.

Emphasis on new buildings in the post-Carnegie era has resulted in better reader environment. If one is driven by a passion for knowledge, as scholars and a few lay people are, one will endure much discomfort, provided he has the book he wants in hand. Uncomfortable chairs, poor light, and lack of heat or ventilation are as nothing when one is enthralled by a book. Yet I do not recommend this kind of monastic discipline for even the hardiest, and we know that the general public is not attracted by such conditions. When a new building is opened, with comfortable chairs and tables, diffused light, soft colors, and books and periodicals on open shelves, library use soars. And when the librarians are bookish, friendly people, then there is heaven-on-earth. I believe in good housekeeping, in work simplification, and in the use of modern devices to relieve drudgery. But I am not in favor of wrapping each book in cellophane or of issuing gloves to the staff. Not a day should pass but that every librarian, in every library on earth, regardless of how high he is in the administrative hierarchy, should handle books. Remember the myth of Hercules and Antaeus? In library work likewise, when a librarian loses physical contact with books, his strength goes. He becomes indistinguishable from administrators anywhere—of stores, hospitals, banks, cemeteries. And he becomes a foreigner to those librarians—still in a majority, thank God—who live, touch, and breathe books, eagerly, lovingly, usefully, rewardingly. And who read books that they may know more, to be able better to serve people, or who read books for simple delight, in order that the world, at once cruel and kind, be made more bearable, more adorable.

Meanwhile, as Aldous Huxley wrote, "Time flows like an unstanched wound," and who among us has read more than a fraction of the books? Draw your own moral, my colleagues, and let us go about our business, our craft, our fine art of librarianship. Books will be read, in spite of unreading librarians. Give us more literate librarians in fine libraries, and the reading of books will be measureless. There is hope in this prospect, and joy.

BOOKMAN IN SEVEN-LEAGUE BOOTS

"Midnight-five" departure from Los Angeles on the third of September, a fever of lights, orchids, and languages, and finally the long runway toward the sea, as Flight 932, the DC-7 *Magnus Viking*, was slowly airborne with its load of gasoline, open-face sandwiches, and people, en route to Scandinavia via the Arctic Circle. English is the cockpit and cabin language of SAS, an English quaintly spoken by mixed crews of Norwegians, Swedes, and Danes, with interludes in their own tongues which are and are not alike. The first book out of my bag was appropriately Jespersen on the English Language, which I savored throughout the twenty-two-hour flight, following his unraveling of our many-threaded tongue.

First stop was Winnipeg in the rainy dawn, oasis in a desert of wheat, fuel stop, leg stretch, chat with a Scottish customs official, and sight of Trans-Canada's maple-leaf

First published in Southwest Review, *Summer 1958.*

planes on the ground. Another long climb for altitude, followed by hours of smooth flight over pinewoods and lakeland, until the earth turned peacock blue, dappled white—Hudson's Bay with icebergs. Then we were over places with names from boyhood's geography by Carpenter, those little blue-gray books which gave one the wide world: Baffin Land, Frobisher Bay, and at sundown the autumn-colored coast of Greenland, where we made a second fuel stop at the American air base of Söndre Strömfjord, seeing the rust-yellow mosses and lichens that grow where the icecap has melted. Another slow climb with a fresh load of gasoline and sandwiches, and then we were over another kind of desert, the great icecap, rose-blue in the last light, pierced by crevasses into which were falling rivulets of melt, then into the cloudcap as night fell.

We made dawn landing at Copenhagen, after a majestic sweep over the harbor, welcomed by a rising cloud of gulls and escorted to the center of town by a parade of cyclists. Paris of the North? A tidier version, more fastidious, as witnessed by the quality of the street-workers, gastronomically grosser, somewhat to Paris what San Francisco is to New York, lacking the enormous vitality which comes from size. While waiting for our hotel room to be readied, we eased stiffness by walking to Frascati's for breakfast, and then took a bus and boat tour of the city. Nothing gives soul to a city as water does, whether it be sea town, lake city, or river port. The boat stopped for tourists to take pictures of the Little Mermaid. Preferring a direct vision of life, we carried no Kodak, and so we gazed at the statue with our eyes, while the others looked at her with their cameras. The *bon mot* of the tour came from the multilingual guide, who referred to Copenhagen's newest hotel, the tall thin Europa, as a "tourist silo." Ours was a small hotel in the Nielshemingsgade, whose only disadvantage was in being opposite the Church of the Holy Ghost, with bells that rang the quarter-hours around the clock. We were up high enough to see midnight fireworks on the closing day of the Tivoli Gardens' summer season.

One evening, after a better than good dinner at Krog's Fish Restaurant, we walked past the squat statue of the aproned Fish Wife, as beautiful in her way as the Little Mermaid, and on to the waterfront where we saw the night boats to Aarhus and Malmö being readied, and a freighter swinging out cases of empty Carlsberg and Tuborg bottles, and full drums of whale oil.

The next morning we crossed Town Hall Square as crowds cheered the arrival of the King and Queen of Denmark and the President of Finland to call on the Mayor of Copenhagen. We wormed to a vantage point and stood for an hour until the royal couple and guest emerged, smiled and waved and were swallowed by a Bentley.

The university quarter, with its bookshops and restaurants and paired students, made me nostalgic for my student years in France. Here I extended my Danish education, commenced earlier by Knud Merrild, Jens Nyholm, Waldemar Westergaard, and Jean Hersholt, by good food and talk with librarians Preben Kirkegaard, Ole Jacobsen, and Carl Thomsen, literate spokesmen for all that we hold good and true. In a restaurant we heard radio music from Helsinki upon the death of Sibelius.

Copenhagen is rich in memorials to Scandinavia's great, other than the Storyteller. A plaque on the wall near the Faculty of Letters told that Holberg had lived there, 1740-1754, while he taught at the University. In the rose garden at the Royal Library we paid homage to a statue of Søren Kierkegaard, glistening in the rain. Sheltered in the Library, one of Europe's great research collections, we were graciously toured by Assistant Librarian Magnussen in the absence of Royal Librarian Palle Birkelund, moved as always by sight of readers fused with the books and manuscripts they were holding, breathing that sweet smell of old books which permeated the erstwhile fortress building. Passing the newspaper stack we saw an old man hopping about like a squirrel after nuts, and were told that he was one of Denmark's eminent scholars, far into his eighties, and one of the few persons allowed the run of the library because of his vast knowledge of what and where. Here in this library where his manuscripts are preserved, I thought of Bishop Grundtvig, who revolutionized Danish education by insisting on the personality of the teacher as being more important than a pedantic curriculum—a revolution needed in the United States where theory, method, and certification are bulldozing the life out of education.

The new Public Library in downtown Copenhagen shares a building with the Ministry for Greenland, and as I entered and looked about admiringly and inquiringly at the fresh decor, I was welcomed and oriented by the coatroom girl. In the literature room I peeked at an oblivious old man's book. It was Zane Grey's *Union Pacific,* in English.

11

We departed from Copenhagen's airport on a rainy morning, and I was sorely tempted to play hooky from schedule and hop to Aarhus, capital of Jutland, that seagirt peninsula from whence comes much of Denmark's strength and sensitivity, remembering a Christmas present in 1945 from Jens Jutlander—a copy of *The Jutland Wind,* a translation of verse from the peninsula. As in all European airports, the intercontinental flights being called also were powerfully seductive—the most of all being one which originated in Oslo, thence to Stockholm, Copenhagen, Frankfurt, Rome, Athens, and Khartoum, terminating in Nairobi.

"I should have liked to rise and go, where the golden apples grow," but instead we went on SAS Flight 561 to London, flying above broken overcast with glimpses of green fields and red roofs, clearing as we crossed the North Sea. We landed at London Airport on a gala Sunday afternoon, crowds lining the promenades to watch the planes come and go—Vickers Viscounts of BEA, a Convair of Aer Lingus, Douglas and Lockheed planes of the American lines and Air France, and our first sight of a Bristol Britannia of BOAC.

Rolling in to Waterloo Air Terminal on a BEA bus, it was apparent that the rhythm of London had not changed, even with traffic at its worst, as, for example, at Hammersmith Broadway, Shepherd's Bush, or Hyde Park Corner. The vehicles at those maelstroms are conducted in a well-mannered and dignified way, compared with New York or Paris.

Seven years earlier we had lived in a Chelsea flat, and though only ten minutes from the heart of London, it was like living in a suburb, up in high rooms overlooking the river and the hills of Kent and Surrey. Now on this briefer stay we lodged at Brown's Hotel in Dover-Albemarle streets, just off Piccadilly, one of London's most quietly elegant hotels with long bathtubs, soft water, and castile soap. The food was English, the service ritualized, to which one adapts or starves. Beef had returned to the menu. No more of 1950's reindeer.

For a few weeks bookshops were my haunt, as I sought to do in that time what had taken me a year before, culminating in the purchase for the state-wide University of California libraries of the 80,000-volume library left by C. K. Ogden, the eccentric scholar who devised Basic English.

Tweed cap, cashmere sweater, Viyella shirts, Church shoes, and a Jaguar fitted me for the road, while my wife collected little handmade woolen birds and beasts to take to all the children at home. We wondered what the maid thought one evening when she came to turn down our beds and found them a menagerie.

The Great North Road from London to Edinburgh is too narrow for the traffic it carries. Although lorry drivers are careful, their number makes speed impossible. There was no hurry. In mid-September frost had not yet blackened the dahlias. There were yellow fields of mustard. Men with chopping knives were waging their ancient war on the encroaching hedges, swinging savagely at the tough stems. Through the hedges crept blackberry vines whose ripe fruit people sought with cautious fingers. Virginia creeper on walls had turned red. Leaves had not yet begun to fall, though beeches were yellowing.

Our itinerary included cathedrals and bookshops. In St. Albans we found the tomb of Bernard de Mandeville, the Elizabethan traveler. Yews in the churchyard were old and beautiful. Elsewhere in town friends lunched us on lamb, green beans, and apple pie, and sold me a great collection of books on early English education. From booksellers near Cambridge I bought such varieties as British detective fiction and a limestone sculpture by Eric Gill. In Oxford we revisited Christ Church to see the John Evelyn collection arranged by Deputy Librarian Hiscock. At Newbury we stayed with friends, and while the girls did more than *talk* about food, the man and I, snug from rain in his garden bookroom, sold and bought books—a great collection of English novels of three centuries and Scottish imprints of the 1600's, happy in one of the best of all symbiotic relationships, that of bookseller and librarian.

On the way north it was too rainy to stop in Peterborough, and we passed through with only a glimpse of the tree-girt Norman abbey. Lincoln was rainy, but we were cozy under the tight roof of the Royal Saracen's Head, and in the misty morning trudged up Steep Hill to see the cathedral on its airy site, with lacy facade and immaculate close, dominated by a statue of Tennyson. We entered as the choir was singing matins, filling the vast space with heavenly sound, saw the Lincoln Imp, and departed. In a bookshop I sought vainly for Lawrence's *Rainbow,* wanting to reread the chapter called "The Cathedral." It was not until we returned to London that I found a copy. Alas, the chapter was more about the inside of Lawrence than of Lincoln.

On the outskirts of York a level-crossing gate arrested us for the passage of a train; and presently it came, running fast in the rain, trailing clouds of steam; not *a* train, but rather The Flying Scotsman, making the 400-mile London-Edinburgh run in eight hours, its red-and-cream coaches drawn by a black, green, and gold engine named "Sir Nigel Gresley," beautiful apparition no sooner seen than gone, swallowed up in the mist, leaving the echo of its banshee whistle.

York meant Scotch broth and a fluffy omelet, a rare Duchess of Newcastle imprint found in a shop in the Stonegate, the apple-green glass of the Minster—and rain. Memorable was a visit to the ruins of Fountains Abbey, the medieval Cistercian monastery near Harrogate, on a clear mild day toward long-shadowed evening after all the trippers had gone, leaving the skeleton arches to the rooks and us. The black birds rose and settled and rose again in raucous protest as we walked on the grass, which grew where once lay flagstone floors. Sheep grazed. I sensed many silent sacred presences, and thought of Browning's "Love Among the Ruins."

> Where the quiet-coloured end of evening smiles,
>   Miles and miles,

> On the solitary pastures where our sheep
>   Half-asleep,
> Tinkle homeward thro' the twilight, stray or stop,
>   As they crop—

North to the border the country begins to thin out and depeople itself, giving a Southwestern American the feeling he gets on approaching his homeland, after exile in the East and Midwest. Stones take the place of shrubs as hedgerow material, hills are domed and barren and given over to sheep; and the Tyne, though by no means an *arroyo seco,* flows sparingly over golden stones as it nears Newcastle and smoke-veiled marriage with salt water. On the grass along the river, white chickens were scattered like confetti. At the Wellington, in a village called Riding Mill, we had one of the best lunches in Britain: lightly fried filet of sole, parsleyed potatoes, a slice of lemon, and ginger beer.

Across river near Corbridge, under High Brunton in a meadow edged with beeches, we found one of the remaining sections of the Roman Wall built by the Emperor Hadrian, a strong point called Brunton Turret, preserved as a national monument. A hundred feet long, five feet thick and as many high, a mass of brute masonry mortared in till Doomsday.

Southbound through the Lake Country we paused overnight at Windermere, finding too many people and not enough country. It was like a city park. Windermere's tributaries were nice though, pouring out of the hillsides clear and cold, and so was the local building stone, all green slate. The Lake Poets were lost in the remembrance that

Beatrix Potter lived and died on her sheep farm across the lake. At this stage of experience I would be tempted to trade Wordsworth for *The Tale of Peter Rabbit,* Coleridge for *Squirrel Nutkin,* with Southey thrown in for *Aunt Jemima Puddleduck.*

Forging southward through the gauntlet of Liverpool and Birmingham, newly partial to Lawrence's hatred of industrialism, we gained sanctuary in County Shropshire, took tea in Shrewsbury, then crossed sodden fields and the swollen Severn at Worcester. Darkness had fallen when we reached our destination, the village of Broadway in the Cotswolds and one of England's loveliest inns, the Lygon Arms, constructed of the yellow local limestone, continuously a hostelry since the time of Shakespeare. Added since, however, were such amenities as running hot water, lighter fare, and Beautyrest mattresses.

Late that afternoon, sight of the wooded hill known as Wenlock Edge had evoked the *Shropshire Lad* and Vaughan Williams' setting of Housman's poems, in the song cycle for tenor and string quartet called *On Wenlock Edge,* and a longing to hear that music again.

> On Wenlock Edge the wood's in trouble;
> His forest fleece the Wrekin heaves;
> The gale, it plies the saplings double,
> And thick on Severn snow the leaves.

The Lord was good to us, for back in London a few days later hear it we did, at one of the great concerts of our life, held in the Royal Festival Hall in honor of Vaughan Williams' eighty-fifth birthday—and that oak of a man was there to hear his music and to bless an overflow crowd, including students in turtle necks and slacks, fully as good to watch in their relaxed mood as the music was to hear. Basil Cameron conducted the *Pastoral Symphony, Job, A Masque for Dancing,* and the song cycle, rearranged for orchestra to accompany the tenor voice. His shadow-dappled music *is* the English countryside and character, as the music of Sibelius typifies Finland.

Emerging into the damp blue murk, seeing barge lights on the river and hearing Big Ben strike ten, the impression was of a Whistler Nocturne. My only regret was that the program had not included the *London Symphony,* his early work which transmuted impressions of the city into music more lasting perhaps even than London.

III

The distance between London and Paris is no measure of the gulf between the two ways of life. The airport limousines of British European Airways and Air France typify the differences. The ride from the Cromwell Road terminal to London Airport was as solemn as the last ride in a hearse. Twenty miles an hour. Silent driver. Passengers whispering, if they spoke at all.

Then the swift flight on BEA's 333, a Vickers Viscount, to Le Bourget and a spreading sense of irresponsibility on the part of employees and passengers. Yet somehow the bus was boarded and away we went, full speed on hard tires over cobbled streets, the driver shouting to no one in particular, the passengers screaming to be heard above